DEAD OF NIGHT

Other books by Cynthia Danielewski:

After Dark
Edge of Night

DEAD OF NIGHT

•

Cynthia Danielewski

AVALON BOOKS

NEW YORK

Published by Thomas Bouregy & Co., Inc.
160 Madison Avenue, New York, NY 10016

Library of Congress Cataloging-in-Publication Data

Danielewski, Cynthia.
    Dead of night / Cynthia Danielewski.
      p. cm.
    ISBN 0-8034-9749-0 (acid-free paper)
    I. Title.

    PS3604.A528D43 2005
    813'.6—dc22
                                            2005009251

PRINTED IN THE UNITED STATES OF AMERICA
ON ACID-FREE PAPER
BY HADDON CRAFTSMEN, BLOOMSBURG, PENNSYLVANIA

For Cathleen—Thank you for your support
and for requesting the story.
&
For my nephew Aiden—welcome to the world!

Chapter One

New York Police Detective Jack Reeves glanced impatiently at his watch as he waited for his wife, Ashley, at the foot of the stairs. "Ashley, we're going to be late," he called up to her.

"I'm coming," she promised.

Jack heard her footsteps before he saw her, and he looked up to catch sight of her coming toward him. His breath caught in his throat. She was beautiful. Her blond hair was elegantly styled, and her long white evening gown highlighted the tan she managed that summer while covering outdoor events as a writer for a society magazine. A job that she accepted after leaving her position as a reporter for the newspaper. A job that allowed her to concentrate on her newest interest in life, that of a would-be mother.

The expression on his face softened as he thought

about the baby that was on the way. Though Ashley was only a few months along in her pregnancy and barely showing, Jack noticed her newfound radiance. It was hard not to. She glowed.

As Ashley descended the stairs, she noticed his expression. Pausing on the bottom step, she asked, "What's wrong?"

Jack reached for her hand and placed a light kiss against it. "Absolutely nothing," he assured her.

"You're looking at me strange."

"I can't help it. You're stunning."

She smiled at his words, touched by the sincerity behind them. She absently reached up to brush a stray lock of his gray-streaked black hair off his forehead, before smoothing a hand against the shoulder of his black tuxedo jacket. "You clean up pretty good yourself."

He returned her smile and reached for her white silk shawl. "Are you ready to go? I told Ryan we would meet him outside the front entrance of the museum at seven," he told her, reminding her of the reason for the evening. They were meeting Jack's partner, Ryan Parks, for the opening of an Egyptian exhibition at the World Museum. Ryan's latest girlfriend, Jane Ramsey, was the senior exhibition designer, and Jack and Ashley had promised to go to the function in support of their friend.

Ashley checked her evening bag. "I'm ready."

"Good. Then let's go," Jack said, escorting her out the front door.

Ashley stood on the porch step while Jack locked the door behind them. "Is Ryan anxious about tonight?"

"Why would he be?"

"I thought he might be nervous on Jane's behalf."

"Jane's a professional. Ryan knows that she's more than capable of pulling off the opening of this exhibition without a hitch."

"I don't doubt her capability. But the museum has a lot riding on it tonight. From my understanding, tonight's going to double as a major fundraising event."

Jack shrugged off the comment. "Jane's good at her job. I'm sure she's used to dealing with the stress that comes along with it."

"I realize that. But I still can't help but be nervous on her behalf. Tonight could make or break her career."

"I'm sure tonight will be a success. From what Ryan told me, there's going to be a lot of people with deep pockets at this event, as well as press coverage. Philanthropists love to get the recognition they think they deserve."

Ashley smiled at Jack's words, and shook her head in mock despair. "You can be so cynical sometimes."

"I prefer to think of it as being realistic," Jack said before placing his hand on the small of her back. "Come on. Let's go."

Twenty minutes later, Jack drove up to the valet parking attendants that were waiting outside the museum's front entrance. Parking the car, he studied the white

Greek Revival-styled mansion that had been recently renovated to become the World Museum, an ambitious venture that people were hoping would change the artistic and cultural landscape of Long Island, New York.

As he looked at the building, he realized just how much effort and work had been put into the project. What was once just a mansion on the North Shore of Long Island, had been completely transformed to become one of the most impressive structures in the area. Ornate columns and decorative pillars framed the entranceway, providing a regal facade that spoke of the architectural design. The elegant gardens on the property presented the perfect setting for the guests to mingle as they waited for the official opening of the doors that would signal that the benefit gala was about to start.

Jack looked at the crowd of people present. Individuals were already standing on the steps and the porch, talking with friends and acquaintances as they waited for the doors to open. Several black-tie refreshment tents had been set up outside, and white-suited waiters and waitresses walked around attending to guests, as the cocktail party that was a prelude to the opening got under way.

"What are you thinking about?" Ashley asked, noticing Jack's preoccupation with the crowd.

"I'm thinking that this will be a long night," he said, already dreading the evening. He had little use for small talk, and even less for people who were filled with their own sense of importance. He wasn't into impressing people, or trying to be something he wasn't. But somehow, looking at the crowd before him, he knew that most of the people present tonight subscribed to both theories. He knew they would go out of their way to outdo each other, both by words and actions, in an effort to gain social status. It was a scene he wasn't comfortable with.

Ashley laughed at his words. "Relax, Jack. The night will go quicker than you think."

He glanced at her with a slight smile. "Somehow, I doubt that," he said with a long suffering sigh before looking back toward the crowd. He had the sudden urge to light a cigarette, and he felt a pang of regret that he had promised Ashley that he would quit smoking. Right now, his craving for a nicotine hit was strong.

"We're here for Jane and Ryan. Just keep those thoughts in mind."

"Believe me, I am," he said as he opened the car door.

Ashley allowed Jack to open her car door before she stepped out. She noticed the news vans set up in the distance, waiting to capture the images and words of the guests. "It looks like this is promising to be some event."

Jack followed her gaze. "Do you still miss reporting?" he asked, knowing that she had had a tough time when she had made the decision to resign from the newspaper. Reporting had been Ashley's life. She took great pleasure in chasing after hardcore news stories. She loved the adrenaline rush she got from the danger. It was a concept that he had a tough time coming to terms with.

Ashley smiled slightly, guessing where his thoughts had gone. Taking his hand in hers, she laid it on her stomach. "Not anymore."

Jack looked at her tenderly. "I'm glad."

She nodded, squeezing his hand slightly in understanding. "Me too."

Jack held her gaze for a moment longer before glancing up as someone caught his attention. "Ryan's here."

"Where?"

"By the entrance."

Ashley turned in that direction, her eyes widening when she finally caught sight of him. "He got a haircut," she said, noticing that his long hair was gone, and replaced by a short conservative cut. The style caused the gray streaks in his brown hair to be less pronounced, making him appear younger than his fifty-three years.

"He had it cut this afternoon."

"Why?" It was the last thing she expected. Ryan had always worn his hair long and clubbed in the back, a remnant from his days in narcotics. It was a style that most men couldn't carry off, but for some reason, she thought it suited Ryan perfectly. That was, until tonight.

Jack smiled, hearing the surprise in her words. "You could hardly expect him to show up here tonight looking like something that the cat had dragged in."

"I never thought he looked bad with long hair."

Jack grunted. "Then you and Ryan are probably the only two who shared that opinion."

Ashley laughed at the disdain in Jack's voice. "Short

hair looks good on him," she admitted, admiring the new look.

"I agree. But be careful not to make him self-conscious about it. I know he had some real reservations about going to the barber."

"I won't even bring up the topic," she assured him before catching sight of a woman walking up to Ryan from behind. "There's Jane."

Jack followed her gaze. "It looks like she just got here."

"Mmm," Ashley murmured, studying the petite woman beside Ryan. Though Ryan was only a little above average in height, he literally dwarfed Jane Ramsey. The sight of them together was a little disconcerting at first glance. Until tonight, Ryan had projected the image of a laid-back hippy, someone who had little use for conventionalism. It was an image that had served him well as an undercover detective on the police force, but it was also a stark contrast to Jane's polished look. Ashley didn't think that she had ever seen Jane where she presented herself as less than perfect. Every hair was perfectly coiffed, every nail was manicured. If there ever seemed to be someone who was the perfect antithesis of Ryan, Jane was it. But there was one thing that Ashley had never doubted. There was one thing that was certain. Ryan cared deeply for the auburn-haired woman who stood by his side. That much was always obvious. The manner in which Ryan treated Jane spoke volumes about his feelings for her. The tender glances he bestowed upon her when she wasn't looking gave insight to his intentions. "They make a nice couple," she observed softly, acknowledging that Ryan's new look more than matched Jane's elegant persona.

"Yeah, they do," Jack agreed. He reached out to gently take Ashley's hand. "Come on. Let's go and say hello."

The moment they reached the other couple, Ryan reached out to kiss Ashley's cheek. "Ashley, you look beautiful," he said.

"Thanks, so do you," she replied softly, her smile telling him without words that she wholeheartedly approved of his new image. She turned and said, "Jane, I love your gown."

"Thanks. I like yours too."

"Thanks. And thank you for inviting us tonight. I've been looking forward to this all week."

"I'm glad you two could make it. I'm a little nervous about tonight. I can use all the moral support I can get."

"Well, you can count on Jack and I to supply it."

"I appreciate that," Jane said before turning to the door. "Come on, let's go inside. The official opening isn't until eight o'clock, but I need to go and do a final run through of the exhibition. You guys can come with me. I want a chance for you to see everything before the crowd is let in."

Ashley breathed a sigh of relief the moment they stepped into the air-conditioned corridor. Though it was late August, the weather that night was much warmer than they had experienced that summer. "It's nice and cool in here."

"It has to be. Otherwise, the workers would pass out from heat exhaustion from the amount of running around they do. Come on. The exhibition room is this way," Jane said, turning to lead the way. Though the museum wasn't open to guests yet, the corridor was bustling with workers rushing about attending to last-minute details. Jane paused outside a heavy wooden door and pushed it open, stepping back to allow the trio to precede her.

"Is it supposed to be this dark?" Jack asked.

"No, it's not." Jane went to the hidden panel of the fuse box. She flicked a couple of switches and the room was instantly flooded with light. "Sorry about that. My assistant was supposed to make sure everything was set to go before we arrived."

"Maybe he got tied up somewhere," Ryan said as he glanced around the room, admiring the details of the exhibition, the care that had been put into the setup. A roped-off platform protected a pyramid display showcasing a life-size gilded wood coffin resting next to a sarcophagus. The coffin glistened under the muted light, lending an air of authenticity to the other artifacts.

"Probably," Jane agreed. "He's pretty reliable. I'm sure he'll have a good explanation of why he wasn't here to get everything ready. Though to be honest, I wish he had called me. I would have planned to get here a little earlier than I did." She looked at Ryan expectantly. "So, what do you think?"

Ryan turned to smile at her reassuringly. "I think it's great," he said before motioning to some jars on a shelf in the display. "What are these for?"

Jane smiled. "They're canopic jars. They were used to hold the internal organs of the embalmed body."

"Oh." Ryan grimaced at the gruesome revelation.

Jane laughed at his expression. "Don't worry. They're only replicas."

"That's a relief."

"You had mentioned that you would have gotten here earlier if you knew your assistant was going to be late. Is there a lot that needs to be done before the doors open?" Jack asked.

"There's not a lot that needs to be done, but a few of the displays need to be adjusted."

"Is there something we can do to help?" Ryan asked.

"No, like I said, it's just a few adjustments," Jane said, beginning to take care of the last-minute preparations.

Jack and Ryan watched from the sidelines while Jane rearranged some items, and Ashley took the opportunity to walk around the room, studying the different artifacts and relics. Some were displayed in glass cabinets, and others stood alone on heavy wooden tables that had been roped off. "This exhibition is great, Jane."

"Thanks," Jane replied, walking up to the display that held the gilded coffin and studying it with a frown.

Ryan walked up beside her and noticed her preoccupation. "What's the matter, sweetheart?"

"Nothing. It's just that I wanted the coffin to be open for the exhibition," she said, stepping forward to open the cover.

Ryan couldn't contain his curiosity, and he looked

inside as soon as the casing gave way. "It's a little dusty inside."

"You're right. I guess Josh didn't get a chance to clean it yesterday. I'm just going to run and get a dust cloth. I'll be right back."

Ryan looked at Ashley and Jack the moment Jane left the room. "She just wants everything to be perfect."

Ashley nodded in understanding. "It will be."

"I think she's a little nervous about tonight," Ryan said, just as a shrill scream filled the air.

"What . . ." Jack said, and immediately took off toward the open doorway, Ryan at his heels.

Running down a long corridor, they saw a group of the museum's workers standing in an alcove. Jack and Ryan pushed their way to the front of the small crowd. They stopped when they saw Jane kneeling on the floor beside a man who lay immobile.

Ryan bent down beside her and reached out a hand to touch her shoulder. "What happened?"

She looked at him with wide eyes. "I opened the maintenance closet to get a dust rag and I found Josh."

"Josh?" Jack questioned, crouching down to feel for the man's pulse.

"Josh Brody. My assistant. Is he all right?"

Jack didn't respond to her question. His full attention was focused on the body.

Ryan watched Jack, not liking the intense look on his partner's face. "Jack? What's the matter?"

Jack lifted his head and looked at Ryan. "He's dead."

Chapter Two

"Dead?" Jane repeated shakily, paling at the words.

Jack noticed her reaction, and his forehead creased with concern. He had been on the force long enough to realize that she was in shock, that she was close to the edge. His eyes met Ryan's in silent communication.

Ryan maintained eye contact with Jack only briefly before he focused his full attention back on Jane. Reaching down, he helped her stand. "Come on, let's get you out of here," he told her gently, concerned for her well-being. He wanted to get her away from the attentive audience in case she lost control. He wanted to give her some privacy to come to terms with finding Josh Brody's body.

Jane didn't want to go with him, she kept staring at Josh's lifeless body lying on the floor. "But Josh—"

"Jack will take care of him," Ryan promised, forcing

her to walk away from the scene, his body blocking her view of the deceased.

Jack watched them leave before glancing at the hovering crowd. He noticed the expressions on the faces around him. The reactions crossed a broad range of emotions, from shock to horror, to just plain curiosity. Knowing that it was imperative that he gain control of the situation, he stood and flashed his detective's badge. "Police Detective Reeves. Please step back from the area," he said, ushering the group away from the body.

Reaching for his cell phone, he dialed the police station to report the possible homicide, all the while watching the faces of the crowd, looking for something, anything, that was suspicious. After getting assurance that backup was on the way, he placed his cell phone back in his pocket, his eyes still on the crowd. He noticed all of them wore the security badge that indicated they were either employed by, or volunteers of the museum.

"Jack? What's going on? What happened?" Ashley asked as she finally was able to force her way through the crowd.

Jack reached out to touch her hand. "Do me a favor, will you?"

"You know I will."

He squeezed her hand slightly in gratitude. "Ryan took Jane into a room over there. Go sit with her and make sure she's okay. I need Ryan out here."

"Sure," she said, her eyes falling to the body on the floor. "Is he—"

"Yes."

She nodded. She didn't need to ask any more questions. She had covered enough homicides during her reporting days to realize that the man was dead. "I'll go sit with Jane," she assured him, knowing that there would be time enough later for questions. She knew her husband better than anybody. And right now, she knew his full attention would be focused on the corpse.

"Thank you."

She nodded once again, and quickly walked away. A few minutes after Ashley left, Ryan came back to join Jack.

"Thanks for sending Ashley to sit with Jane."

Jack shrugged off the words. "No thanks are necessary. She wants to help in any way she can."

"I know."

"Is Jane all right?"

"As well as can be expected."

"I have to admit, I thought for sure she was going to pass out."

"Yeah, finding out that Josh was dead hit her hard."

"These type of circumstances would hit anybody hard."

"I know." Ryan looked at the crowd. "How did you want to proceed?"

"We have to get these people isolated and begin questioning them. Maybe someone noticed something suspicious," Jack told him, keeping his voice low.

"I'll get a list with people's names and phone numbers. At least then, we'll have a starting point."

Jack nodded. "I'll inform security that nobody else sets foot inside this museum tonight except our own people."

Ryan glanced at his watch. "How long before they get here?" he asked, knowing without being told that Jack had already placed the call to the station.

"Any minute now. They're sending the patrol cars over that were in the area to control the mob outside, and the crime scene investigators should be here shortly. The security guards can watch the entrances to ensure that no curious spectators make their way inside."

"Do you think Josh's death was the result of a robbery?" Ryan asked, thinking of the valuable museum pieces that would be worth a fortune on the open market.

"Possibly," Jack replied, knowing it was a feasible explanation. "But right now, I think the best thing to do is to get everybody isolated so that we can determine exactly what happened."

"I'll get everyone here situated in the lounge area. At least there are tables and chairs set up. It should make the interview process go a lot more smoothly."

"Sounds good. As soon as our backup arrives, I'll send the uniformed officers in to relieve you, and you can meet me back here, and we'll start to sort through this mess."

"Okay." Ryan took out his badge and turned to the crowd to address them. "Ladies and gentlemen, I'm Detective Parks and I'm asking for your cooperation. If you'll follow me," he directed. He led the way to the lounge, his voice carrying back to Jack as he explained to everyone the procedures the police were going to be implementing, and what they could expect.

The moment Ryan cleared the area, Jack turned to the three security men who stood off to the side. "If you three could cover the entrances, I would appreciate it. Nobody enters or leaves without my authorization, with the exception of the police."

The guards nodded, and walked off to attend their posts.

Jack waited until they left before looking back down at the body. Crouching, he studied the victim, searching for anything that would constitute foul play. He could find nothing. There were no bloodstains on his clothing, no marks visible on his face, neck, or hands. Nothing about the man gave any clue as to what had happened. Even his facial expression hinted little.

Looking to the open doorway of the maintenance closet that the man was found in, he glanced inside. The cleaning supplies were arranged in an orderly fashion. There didn't appear to be anything out of place that would suggest some sort of a struggle or altercation had taken place.

As he looked inside the highly organized area, he came to the realization that Josh Brody was already dead or on the verge of death when his body had been placed inside the small room. He had to be. It was the only theory that made sense. There was no other explanation for the room to be so clean and organized and untouched.

Jack was just rising to his feet to walk into the closet

when some uniformed officers joined him. He brought them up to speed on what had occurred, and directed them to the lounge where Ryan had moved the crowd so that they could assist with obtaining statements. As soon as they left, he stepped inside the closet.

He was studying the interior floor for possible evidence when he noticed the tip of something black protruding from underneath a bottom shelf. Frowning, he took a pen out of his pocket and carefully placed the tip on the object to pull it towards him, realizing as he did that it was a leather glove.

"What's that?" Ryan asked as he walked up beside him.

Jack turned to look at him. "A glove."

Ryan frowned and crouched down. "Where did you find it?"

"Under the shelf."

"It looks like the type of glove someone would wear in the winter. The museum wasn't open in the winter months," Ryan pointed out, thinking of the implications of the find.

"I know."

"That would mean that there's a possibility that this glove might have something to do with Josh Brody's death."

"I have a feeling that it's more than a possibility." Jack stood and motioned to one of the officers in the hallway. "Get me something to put this in, will you?"

The officer retrieved a paper clasp envelope from the guard booth and handed it to Jack.

"Thanks," Jack said, picking up the glove with the tip of the pen and moving it carefully into the envelope.

"Maybe there'll be some fibers or hair on the glove," Ryan suggested.

"Let's hope so." Jack motioned with his chin in the direction of the lounge. "How's it going in there?"

"Everybody seems a little shocked."

"That's to be expected."

Ryan sighed. "Yeah, I know. A dead body was the last thing I expected to find here tonight. Do you think this is a homicide or something less sinister?"

"The body was stuffed into this closet. What do you think?"

"I admit, there doesn't seem to be another explanation other than homicide to explain how the guy's body ended up in here. Finding this glove goes a long way to support that theory."

"I agree. If the museum had been open a little longer, there might be a plausible explanation of how the glove ended up where it did. But considering it only opened this past April . . ." He looked around the small room once more. "Do you think this room is usually locked?" he suddenly asked.

"Jane said the door was locked, and I would imagine that it would always have to be," Ryan replied, gesturing to the chemicals stacked on the shelves. "Most of these chemicals are hazardous. I don't think the museum can take any chances that some of them might be removed. For one thing, they couldn't afford to take the risk that some of the museum's artifacts could be destroyed if the chemicals came into contact with them."

"True. And then there's the liability if someone accidentally ingested any of the compounds, or received some kind of chemical burn."

Ryan lifted a shoulder expressively. "I doubt anyone would be careless enough to take any of the risks we just mentioned."

"Hmm," Jack murmured, his attention turning to the doorway and the sound of footsteps. He motioned with his chin to several of the crime scene investigators that had arrived. "Let me go and talk to them."

As soon as Jack was through, he returned to Ryan's side.

"All right. Now that they're about to get started on the search, maybe one of us should go and check on Ashley and Jane," Jack said.

"I already checked on them. I stopped in after the officers relieved me in the lounge. Ashley's fine." Ryan knew of Jack's concern for Ashley's health since they found out she was pregnant.

Jack nodded, relieved. "Is Jane any better?"

"Not by much. Ashley's trying to get her to calm down a little."

"If anybody can, it would be her."

"I know. I'm grateful for her support."

"Like I said earlier, Ashley wants to help in any way she can. She knows that finding the body had to be a shock for Jane," Jack said, glancing toward the room that Jane and Ashley were waiting in. "Jane will be okay. She's strong."

"Yeah, I know," Ryan said, his words sounding more convincing than his tone of voice.

"Just out of curiosity, did Jane happen to say anything that would possibly shed some light on this mess?"

"Not much. She just said that Josh Brody was supposed to stay late last night getting everything ready for the opening of the exhibition."

"The security log should tell us what time he actually left."

Ryan sighed and ran a weary hand across the back of his neck. "I also stopped by the security office on the way back from the lounge."

"And?"

"And, they don't have an entry regarding the time Josh Brody left the museum."

Jack's eyes narrowed. "Did they have an entry for when he arrived at the museum?"

"They have only one entry for him yesterday. It was at eleven in the morning."

"It sounds like the guy never left the building."

"That's the way it looks."

Jack glanced toward the security desk in the front entryway of the museum. He noticed a few high-tech monitoring systems, but nothing that really stood out as state-of-the-art technology. Nothing that stipulated every possible avenue had been covered in protecting the artifacts of the museum, many of which were priceless. "How good do you think their security measures are around here?"

Ryan shrugged. "Jane always made it seem like the security was very stringent when she mentioned it in the past."

"This is a small museum compared to the ones in the city."

"Yeah, but that wouldn't mean the security measures were any less efficient."

"That remains to be seen."

"Granted. I'm only making the comment based on what I heard. If security wasn't doing their job, Jane had no knowledge of it."

Jack was silent for a moment. "What time did Jane leave last night?"

"She said around seven."

"And Josh Brody was here when she left?"

"Yes. She said he told her that he wanted to stay and finish some loose ends."

"And she felt comfortable with him doing that by himself?" Jack asked, knowing that Jane was the senior designer of the exhibit. He was a little curious about why she would leave the museum if the exhibition wasn't completed. He thought about Ashley's remarks earlier. She had been right on one thing. The successfulness of the exhibition could make or break Jane's career. That fact couldn't be ignored. So the question remained, why was Jane willing to leave the outcome of such an important event in Josh Brody's hands?

"She said she had the utmost confidence in his abilities," Ryan said.

"How long was he her assistant?"

"From my understanding, just since the museum opened. Why?"

"Just curious. It seems like she put a lot of faith in his abilities to ensure that this exhibition was perfect," Jack said, studying Ryan as he said the words, wondering how he would react to the comment.

"I know. But she insists that he was more than qualified to put the finishing touches on everything. She said they had worked long enough together, and had enough meetings on the subject to ensure that they were both on the same wavelength."

"I guess that makes sense."

Ryan's eyes met Jack's. "I have no reason to doubt her," he said, knowing instinctively where Jack was going with the comment. He knew Jack was considering Jane as a possible suspect in what had occurred. But, he couldn't get upset with him. He knew it was a reasonable inference considering the circumstances. He knew Jack wasn't making a personal attack against Jane.

Jack nodded, relieved that he could detect no animosity in Ryan's words, in his body language. He knew his comment could have been translated as being inflammatory, especially since Ryan had a personal relationship with Jane. He knew once emotions were involved, common sense almost always took a backseat. "I meant no offense," he assured Ryan. "I'm just thinking out loud."

"I know. You didn't say anything that I didn't already think about."

Jack was silent for a moment, his attention diverted to the body. He motioned with his chin to Brody. "We don't have too much to work with here. There's no blood, no bruises, no disturbance."

"All of which leads us to no obvious answer."

"Right now, the only thing that's obvious is that foul play was involved."

"Yeah, I have to agree. Jane said he fell out of the closet immediately after she opened it. That would mean that he had to have been near the door."

"Which means that the door had to be closed the whole time he was in there. Otherwise, somebody would have noticed him," Jack said as he walked back toward the closet. He looked at the door handle. "Maybe we'll be able to pick up some prints from the doorknob. At the very least, we'll be able to determine if Josh Brody touched the knob to either get into, or out of the closet," he added, just as he caught sight of the new captain of police, Ed Stall, coming toward them.

Ed nodded in greeting. "Gentlemen."

"Hi, Ed," Jack greeted.

"Ed," Ryan acknowledged.

"I heard we found a body."

"That's right," Ryan replied. "The man's name is Josh Brody. He's Jane's assistant."

Ed's eyebrows rose slightly. "Any idea on what happened?"

Jack shrugged. "No, nothing as of yet. The body was found in this maintenance closet."

"Doesn't sound like the guy died of natural causes if the body was hidden."

"No, it doesn't," Jack agreed.

Ed looked at Ryan. "Is there anybody you know of who may have had a possible motive to take the man out of the picture?"

"Not offhand."

"Did you talk to Jane yet?" Ed asked.

"Just briefly. She's extremely upset right now. Ashley's sitting with her at the moment."

Ed nodded in understanding. "What about the other employees? Did they see anything?"

"Nobody came forward with any information as of yet," Jack said.

"So, we have nothing to go on."

"No, but the investigation is just starting," Jack replied.

"There were a lot of people scheduled to be here tonight," Ryan added. "It will take a while to see if we can make some sort of connection between one of them and Brody's death."

"How many people are in the building now?" Ed asked.

"About twenty-five," Ryan replied.

"And do we know if anything is missing? Are we dealing with a robbery gone wrong?"

"There's nothing apparent that's showing," Jack responded. "No ransacking anyway. But to be honest, the museum will have to do a full inventory before we'll have that answer."

Ed looked around at the search team going through the museum with a fine-toothed comb. "What about the criminalists? Did they find anything?"

"They just started the search," Ryan said.

Ed nodded. "They're thorough. If there's anything here, they'll find it. We just have to give them some time to do their job."

"I agree," Jack said.

"Are the workers who were in the building when the body was discovered being questioned?"

"They're in the lounge now with some uniformed officers."

"Good. I already gave instructions to the officers outside to question everybody out there," Ed said.

"How many officers?" Jack asked, knowing that the crowd expected for the cocktail party was huge.

"About fifteen to handle the crowd outside, and three by the barricade set up by the museum's entrance to take names and numbers. If we need more resources, I'll bring them in," Ed replied before looking at one of the criminalists who was working by the doors to the Egyptian exhibition. "It looks like he may have found something," he said, noticing the man take a sample of something off the floor. Walking over to the guy, he bent down to study the area that he was processing. "What did you find?"

The criminalist didn't look up from his task. "Some kind of liquid was spilled here."

Chapter Three

J ack frowned at the man's words and took a few steps forward. Crouching down, he studied the area. "Liquid?"

"Yeah. The residue is from some kind of sticky substance," the criminalist replied absently as he diligently collected the sample.

Ryan considered the man's words. "They don't allow food or beverages in the main area of the museum. And definitely not by any of the exhibitions."

Jack glanced in his direction. "Do they have a cafeteria in the building?"

"They have a small café in the back, but I don't believe they allow anything to be transported out of the immediate area," Ryan replied.

Jack stood up and stretched his legs. "Do you think that rule applies to the workers as well?"

"I know it does. I've heard Jane complain about it on more than one occasion, especially when they're setting up."

"There's always a chance that somebody broke that rule," Ed interjected.

Jack looked down at the area that was being processed. "I would say that it's a foregone conclusion that somebody did. And whoever it was did a shoddy job of cleaning up the residue of whatever it was they spilled."

The criminalist finished collecting samples and stood. "We should have the report on this sometime tomorrow."

Ryan looked down at the spot that had just been processed before glancing over at the maintenance closet. "What do you think the chances are that the spill on the floor and Josh Brody's body being in the closet are somehow connected?"

"I would say it's a good guess," Jack replied.

"I agree. It's a reasonable assumption," Ed said.

"Do you think it's possible that Josh spilled something and his death occurred when he went to the closet to get the cleaning supplies to take care of the mess?" Ryan asked, trying to think of possible scenarios.

"Anything's possible. But we don't have enough information to confirm any one theory," Jack replied.

Ed's gaze encompassed both men. "We'll have to wait and see what evidence actually surfaces."

Jack was quiet for a moment as he studied the crowd outside the front door being interviewed by police. Looking across to Ed, he asked, "How was the crowd outside when you arrived?"

Ed shrugged. "Impatient. Curious," he said, his attention diverted back to what was going on inside the museum. He watched as the crime scene technicians boxed the items that had been stored in the maintenance closet. "We're going to have some mess to sort through."

"That's always the case," Jack said distractedly as he glanced at his watch. "What time do you think the coroner will get here?"

"He should be arriving shortly. I called his office on my way over here. They assured me he was on his way."

"Once the body's removed, we'll have an easier time maneuvering our way around here."

There was a moment of silence while Ed looked at Jack and Ryan. "I take it you two have no problem being assigned to the case?"

"Was there ever any doubt?" Ryan asked.

Ed shrugged. "Honestly, a little. I need to know that you can handle this case without reservations. That there won't be a conflict of interest on your end," he said, referring to Ryan's relationship with Jane Ramsey, and her connection to the museum, to the victim.

Ryan's eyes met Ed's. "There won't be any conflict," he assured him, not hesitating in his reply.

"Good," Ed said before he gestured to the front door. "Here comes the coroner now."

Thirty minutes later, the body had been removed and Jack, Ryan, and Ed stood in the Egyptian exhibition room while the items on display were thoroughly dusted for fingerprints.

Ed looked toward the doorway, searching for the mechanism that would enable the museum to keep track of everybody's coming and goings. With the exception of a security camera, he didn't see anything. "It's too bad they don't have some kind of security system set up to record the ID of everybody who enters the room."

"Unfortunately, the museum relies on their security personnel for that. I don't think they keep track of who enters every exhibition area. Only the people that enter and leave the museum," Ryan said.

"We'll have to get access to the film from the security cameras. Maybe that will reveal something," Ed remarked.

Jack nodded in agreement. "We'll also have to run background checks on everybody who was here yesterday and today."

"I'll get a copy of the security log and film before I leave here tonight. I can at least get the ball rolling on that. Maybe we'll get lucky and something will be on the film," Ed said.

"That would be a big help," Jack said just as he heard the sound of voices out in the corridor. He automatically turned in that direction, watching as a gray-haired gentleman entered the room, arguing loudly with a security guard who stood by his side. Jack recognized the guard as one of the three he had seen earlier when Josh

Brody's body had first been discovered. He looked at the guard expectantly, waiting for him to explain the interruption, to explain the man's presence.

The security guard, whose badge read Dane Trevor, stepped forward immediately. "This is Andrew Carstair. He's the curator of the museum."

At the introduction, Jack stepped forward, his hand outstretched. "Mr. Carstair. I'm Detective Reeves." Then he introduced Ryan and Ed.

"I heard Josh Brody is dead. What can you tell me about what happened?" he asked bluntly, his demeanor both professional and concerned.

"His body was discovered in a maintenance closet," Jack said, watching the man's facial expression as he made the statement, searching for any sign of unease, anything that would flag suspicion.

"The maintenance closet?"

"That's right," Ryan confirmed.

Andrew's gaze encompassed all three men. "How did he die?"

"We're not sure yet," Jack replied.

"Was it a robbery?"

"That remains to be seen. And in actuality, in order for us to determine exactly what happened, we'll need your assistance," Jack said.

"My assistance?" Andrew questioned, his eyebrows shooting up at the words.

Jack watched his reaction carefully. "Yes. We'll need a detailed inventory of the museum's artifacts. A comparative listing of what should be here, and what actually is here."

"Of course."

"Can you tell if anything looks out of place?" Ryan asked.

Andrew looked around the room. "The opening of the exhibition tonight was supposed to be our big event. And at first glance, everything that should be here, is here. At least in this room."

"We'll need an actual confirmation of that," Jack said. "We also need a rundown on the other exhibitions on display. I'd like a detailed listing of your volunteers, as well as your employees. The list should contain phone numbers and addresses, as well as work schedules."

"It's summer. A lot of people are on vacation," Andrew said.

"I still want their names. If your security is what it should be, we'll be able to cross-reference who's been in the building during the last twenty-four hours."

Andrew was silent for only a moment while he contemplated the request. "I'll get it for you as soon as possible."

"We would appreciate that," Jack said.

Andrew nodded. "Our director of security, Bryce Cumming, should be here momentarily. Maybe he'll be able to be of some assistance."

"Was he on site today?" Ed asked.

"No, he had a meeting in the city. But he was supposed to be here tonight," Andrew replied.

"We'll want to see him as soon as possible," Jack remarked.

"Of course. I'm sure Bryce wants to talk to you too."

"Is he aware of what happened here tonight?" Ryan asked.

"No. He just knows there was some trouble. That's all that I was told on the phone," Andrew replied. He paused for a moment before asking, "Where's Jane?"

"She's in another room," Ryan answered.

"Is she okay?"

"She's the one who found Josh Brody. I'm sure you can understand just what type of shock that was."

"Can I see her?"

"Of course. But we'd like a few more minutes of your time first," Ed said.

"I'll help in any way I can."

Ed nodded. "We appreciate that. Just out of curiosity, why were you so late in getting here tonight? Weren't you going to be here for the opening of the exhibit?"

"I was, but I had car trouble. Otherwise I would have been here much earlier."

"What kind of car trouble?" Jack asked.

Andrew frowned at the question. "The battery was dead."

"Were you here last night?" Ed asked.

"Yes, until about eight o'clock."

"Did you see Josh Brody when you were here?" Ryan questioned.

"I ran into him in the cafeteria."

"Was he alone?" Jack asked.

"Yes. Yesterday was a very hectic day for everybody. I'm afraid everybody is pretty much on their own for meals when we're getting an exhibition ready."

"The cafeteria was open last night?" Ed asked.

"We had no servers or cooks here, but there's a refrigerator and microwave available for employee use."

"How stringent is your policy regarding food or beverages leaving the cafeteria?" Jack asked.

"It's not allowed."

"Have you ever known anybody to break that rule?" Ed asked.

Andrew opened his mouth to respond, when something gave him pause. "Actually, I'm aware of one instance."

"Who was it that broke policy?" Ryan questioned.

"It was Josh Brody."

"What happened?" Ed asked.

Andrew shook his head. "Nothing really. I just gave him a warning not to do it again. He seemed to understand the message. I never pursued it further."

Ryan nodded. "How was Brody yesterday when you saw him?"

"What do you mean?" Andrew asked, seeking clarification on the question.

"How was his demeanor? Did he say anything to you? Anything that you found odd or disturbing?"

"No. We shared just normal small talk. Nothing major and not anything of any substance."

"He was his normal self?" Ryan persisted.

"As far as I could tell. If there was something

wrong, I couldn't detect it. He seemed excited about the opening."

Ryan nodded and reached inside his jacket for one of the business cards he always carried. He held it out to Andrew. "Here's my card. If you can think of anything that you believe may be relevant to this investigation, please call me."

Andrew reached out to take the card. He glanced briefly at it before pocketing it. "I will."

"Thanks."

"It's not a problem," Andrew assured him before turning toward the door. "I'd like to go and check on Jane. Would it be all right?"

Ryan nodded. "Of course. That's all the questions we have for now."

"If you need me for anything else . . ."

"We'll know where to find you," Ryan added.

"Then I'll see you in a bit," Andrew replied as he walked from the room.

As soon as Andrew left, Ryan turned to Jack and Ed. "Well? What did you think of him?"

Ed shrugged. "He seemed okay. At least he appears to be willing to cooperate with us."

"Yeah, he does," Jack agreed. "And time will tell how helpful he'll be in helping us determine exactly what happened to Josh Brody."

"With any luck, he'll give us the list of personnel sometime tomorrow," Ryan said.

"We'll just have to apply a little pressure if he looks like he's going to procrastinate," Ed interjected.

"I agree," Jack said, glancing at his watch. "Look, I'm going to go and check on Ashley and see if she's doing okay."

Ryan smiled slightly at Jack's concern. "She's pregnant, Jack. She's not sick. You seem to forget that she used to thrive in this type of environment," he said, making a reference to Ashley's days as a reporter.

"Believe me, I didn't forget that. I just want to make sure she's feeling okay."

"I'm sure she's fine," Ryan said.

"I just want to be sure. And besides, there's another reason I want to go and talk to her."

"Why?" Ed asked.

"I can guarantee you that her instincts from her reporting days are kicking in. She might have found out some information that could be useful. You two stay here and see if anything surfaces that might help with the investigation."

"Not a problem," Ryan said. "Check that Jane is okay while you're there?"

"You know I will."

Chapter Four

Jack heard the sound of voices as he walked toward the room where Ashley and Jane were waiting. Looking inside, he saw Jane standing in a corner with Andrew Carstair. They were talking in low, soft voices.

As he looked on, something about seeing them standing beside each other peaked his curiosity. But he wasn't exactly sure what it was. There was just something about their mannerisms. Something about the closeness that they seemed to share. He tried to hear what their conversation was about, but he couldn't make out the words. Their voices were too low, too garbled.

Glancing over at Ashley sitting by herself on the other side of the room, he caught her eye and motioned her outside. He took her hand as soon as she reached his side. "How are you feeling?" he asked, his eyes going over her face, over her figure, assuring himself that she was okay, that the events of the evening hadn't taken too much of a toll on her.

Ashley smiled at his concern. It was a sentiment that he expressed repeatedly since the day he had found out about her pregnancy. She got the distinct impression that it was something she was going to have to get used to. Jack seemed to equate her condition with helplessness. And while she would be the first to admit that his over-protectiveness was a bit too much at times, she would also be the first to admit that she found his concern touching, even endearing. "All right," she assured him softly, squeezing his hand in reassurance.

"Truth?" he asked, his eyes searching hers, looking for something that would back up her words.

"Truth."

He nodded, relaxing somewhat after her answer, after his own eyes convinced him that she was okay. "How's Jane?" he asked, looking back into the room to where she stood almost head to head with Andrew Carstair as they talked. He couldn't help but frown at the sight. Their actions were too personal, almost intimate.

Ashley followed his gaze. "She's still shaken up. I can't say that I really blame her."

"No, I know."

"There's nothing going on between Jane and Andrew Carstair," she told him softly, having an idea of how his mind worked, of where his thoughts had wandered to. "She's completely devoted to Ryan."

"I know she is. But you have to admit, Jane and Andrew seem very close."

"It's platonic."

"Maybe now it is," Jack countered.

Ashley smiled slightly at the cynicism in Jack's voice. His cynicism about life was part of who he was. It was an ingrained part of his personality, of his perception of mankind. She didn't think it was something she would be able to break him of. Old habits died hard. And in truth, Jack's cynicism about people, about life, was part of what made him such a good cop. He was never taken in by outward appearances. "How's the investigation going?" she asked, drawing his attention momentarily away from Jane and Andrew.

Jack expelled a small breath and shrugged. "Slowly."

"Did the coroner come yet?"

"Yeah, a while ago."

"Did he make any comments regarding any theories about what happened?"

"Not yet. We should hopefully know something by tomorrow."

She nodded. "I think Jane will be feeling better by tomorrow. She'll probably feel up to talking a little more about Josh Brody."

"I hope so. I'm counting on her input to help us determine exactly what happened to the man."

"I'm sure she'll be better able to cope tomorrow. She just needs a good night's sleep to come to terms with everything."

"I'm sure you're right," Jack said, not wanting to get into a debate with her.

Ashley moved a little further away from the open

doorway, out of earshot of Jane and Andrew. "A police officer came to take our statements a little while ago."

Jack was somewhat surprised that the officer took it upon himself to interview them without himself or Ryan present. "Oh?"

"Relax. He was very professional, very understanding."

"You should have asked for me. He would have waited until I got here," he told her, not liking the idea of them being interviewed without his knowledge, and without his presence.

"There was no need. It was a brief interview. Jane was pretty limited in what she could tell him."

"Did you hear her statement?"

"Yes. Basically she just told him the details that led up to her finding Josh Brody's body."

"Was she calm when she made the statement?"

Ashley thought about his question seriously. "I would say that she was in control of her emotions."

"Good. Ryan's very concerned about her."

"She'll be fine. You can tell Ryan that. I imagine he's probably going crazy with worry."

"He knows she's in good hands with you."

Ashley smiled slightly at the compliment. "Thank you."

Jack was quiet for a moment before asking, "Did Jane say anything to you at all privately?"

"Not much. Not anything relating to Josh Brody's death anyway. I think she's still trying to come to terms with finding him dead."

Jack looked over to where Andrew was talking to Jane. "How did they react to seeing each other?" he asked, wondering at the relationship between them. As much as he hated to admit it, Jane's actions were going to have to come under scrutiny. And so were Andrew's.

Ashley studied the couple across the room, thinking seriously about the question. "They actually greeted each other like old friends."

"What do you mean?"

She lifted a shoulder expressively. "They seem very comfortable with each other. Like they share a lot of history."

"Did you pick up any vibes from either of them?"

"Nothing telling. Right now, they both seem to be in mourning."

He nodded, and after a moment, he shifted his attention and focus back to Ashley. Reaching out, he tenderly moved a stray piece of hair away from her face. "Are you sure you're holding up okay? You're not tired?"

She laughed slightly. "I'm always tired lately. You know that."

"I know. I just want to make sure that tonight isn't too much for you."

"I'm fine," she assured him.

He held her gaze for a moment. "I'm afraid it will be a couple of more hours before I'm through. If you want, you can take the car and head home. I'll catch a ride with Ryan."

She quickly discarded his suggestion. "No, that's okay. I'd like to stay. For Jane's sake if nothing else."

"Are you sure?"

"Positive."

"Okay. Then I'm going to go and finish taking care of business. Give a shout if you need me."

"I will."

"I'll see you later," he said, turning to walk away.

Ashley waited until he turned a corner before she walked back into the room.

Ten minutes later, Jack walked back into the exhibition room where Ryan and Ed waited.

"Well?" Ryan asked.

"Jane's fine."

"And Ashley?" Ed asked.

"She's fine too."

"You were gone awhile," Ryan said.

Jack shrugged. "Since everything was under control, I took the opportunity to stop off at the lounge on the way back here."

Ed nodded slightly in approval. "How's it going in there?"

"They have statements from most of the people. According to the officers, everybody seems more than willing to cooperate."

"That's good," Ed remarked.

"Yeah, it is," Jack murmured, his hand reaching up to rub the back of his neck wearily, while he looked at Ryan. "They already took statements from Jane and Ashley," he said, wondering how Ryan would react to the fact that he wasn't with Jane during the process.

Ryan's eyes shot up to meet his. "They did?"

"Relax. Ashley said the officer basically handled them with kid gloves."

Ryan nodded. "I wish Jane or Ashley would have called us."

"I'm sure they would have if they felt they needed our assistance," Jack murmured, looking around the room. "How did everything go here?"

"Nothing new showed," Ryan replied.

"And in the rest of the building?" Jack asked.

"They're still searching, but so far, nothing has been reported," Ed answered.

Jack looked at the criminalists who were industriously searching for prints, or anything else that could possibly be considered as evidence. "With any luck, they'll complete the autopsy on Josh Brody by morning. At least then we'll have a better idea of what exactly we're dealing with."

"I agree. And with that, we'll have to apply a little pressure to Andrew Carstair to complete the museum's inventory. Somebody went to great pains to hide Josh Brody's body out of plain sight," Ryan said.

"That alone indicates that the guy didn't die of natural causes," Ed said.

"There's no visible sign of trauma to the body," Ryan pointed out.

"True. But the toxicology report is going to tell us a lot about what happened," Jack replied.

"Like you said, we'll have a much better picture of everything tomorrow," Ed stated. "But as for tonight, we just need to make sure that we cover all the bases so that we don't lose any advantage point in solving this."

"Talking to the director of security would go a long way in accomplishing that," Ryan said.

"Yeah, it would," Ed agreed. "Andrew Carstair said he was on his way. The man should be here shortly."

"I find it very strange that all the major players at the museum seem to be running late on such an important night," Jack said.

"Yeah, I was thinking the same thing," Ryan admitted.

"Ditto," Ed said.

"So far, everyone has been able to offer an explanation for their absence. It'll be interesting to hear Bryce Cumming's account for his whereabouts," Jack said.

"Maybe this is him now," Ryan said, turning to look at the door as the echo of footsteps came closer to the room, followed by the sight of a tall, burly man stepping through the threshold.

"I'm Bryce Cumming," the man said, his voice steady and strong.

Ryan stepped forward. "I'm Detective Parks and this is my partner, Jack Reeves, and Captain Ed Stall."

Cumming nodded in acknowledgement. "I just saw Andrew Carstair in the hallway."

"I take it he told you what happened?" Jack asked, studying the man curiously, noticing the total professionalism of his attire, the seriousness of his demeanor.

"He told me that my brother is dead."

Chapter Five

There was a moment of stunned silence while the man's words rang through the air.

"Your brother?" Jack asked, recovering first from the revelation.

"Half-brother to be exact," Bryce said.

"Nobody mentioned your relationship to Josh," Ryan said slowly, trying to make sense out of the admission.

Bryce expelled a harsh breath. "Nobody knew."

"Was that by accident or design?" Ed asked.

"We thought it best to keep the relationship quiet."

"Why?" Ryan asked.

"Security reasons. Josh desperately wanted this job. If anybody realized that we were related, there's every reason to believe that he would have been overlooked for the post."

"I take it that you were the one responsible for running his background check," Jack said, trying to figure out exactly what happened, how this information had remained a secret.

"That's correct."

"I'm sorry for your loss," Jack told him, not knowing how his words would be perceived. He couldn't really tell if Bryce and Josh had been close, or if their relationship was strictly by blood. By the man's apparent stoic nature, he would guess it was the latter, but he couldn't really be sure.

"Thank you."

"Keeping your relationship a secret must have been tough," Ryan said in an attempt to get the man to open up.

Bryce shrugged. "Not really. Unfortunately, we really didn't know each other that well. As you probably noticed, we have different last names. After my parents divorced, I lived with my father, and my mother remarried and moved away. She died when Josh was just a baby, so I never knew him."

"Did you know of his existence?" Jack asked.

"I found out about our relationship when he applied for the position at the museum. Running his background check actually. When I discovered the possible relationship, I questioned him and discovered that we shared the same mother."

"How did he react to the news?" Ed asked.

Bryce shrugged again. "About the same as me. We were a little leery toward each other."

"That's understandable," Ryan said.

Bryce looked over at Ryan. "I'm forty-five, Josh was thirty-eight. You don't cross that many years without having reservations about the existence of each other."

"Did you resent Josh's presence?"

"You mean because we shared the same mother?"

"Yes."

"As I said, my parents were divorced and my mother passed away a long time ago. There was no resentment against Josh."

"Yet you didn't want people to know about your relationship," Ed pushed, trying to clarify what the man was saying.

Bryce shrugged. "There was no reason for anybody to. Josh and I never had a relationship. The reality is, if the background check was any less thorough, our relationship would have never come to light. People finding out that we were half-brothers would have only hurt Josh's chance at expanding his career, at least here. The museum has a policy prohibiting relatives from working together."

"We appreciate your honesty now," Jack said.

"I want to help in any way I can to find out what happened to Josh."

Jack nodded. "I understand. And we're going to need to take you up on your offer. If you have the time right now, I'd like to get a glimpse of your security control room."

Bryce didn't hesitate in his response. "Sure. Follow me," he said, turning to leave the room.

Jack, Ryan, and Ed followed Bryce down a long corridor until they came to a steel door at the end of the hall. They watched as Bryce reached into his pocket for his keys.

"This is it," Bryce said, unlocking the door and ushering them inside.

Jack looked around at the numerous video monitors set up against the wall giving real-time feed about what was going on in the museum. "What type of logging devices do you use for museum personnel?"

Bryce gestured to the manuals resting on a bookcase. "Each of the employees, as well as volunteers, are required to manually sign in and out at the guard booth every time they enter or leave the premises."

"Do you cover all the entrances of the museum to ensure that the procedure is adhered to?" Jack asked.

"Yes. As a rule, all doors but the main lobby's entrance remain locked. I also have security guards posted throughout the museum to make sure that there are no security breaches."

"You don't have a palm scanner or security badge system?" Ryan asked.

"No. Everybody is assigned a badge, but not for scanning purposes. Badges have been known to become lost or stolen. I realize that our methods might seem a little antiquated, but the museum doesn't have the funds to invest in palm-scanning technology. Especially since we have so many volunteers. Maybe if our payroll was bigger we would be able to justify the cost, but as it stands now, we decided to go with the tried and true method of face to face contact."

"Have you ever had any problems in the past with security?" Ryan asked.

"None."

"At all?" Ed persisted.

"Not with theft, not with employees, and not with volunteers. Our background check policy is pretty stringent. I can get you a copy of our records if you think it would help."

"It would," Jack acknowledged.

"I'll have my secretary make copies tomorrow morning and I'll drop them by the station if that's okay."

"We would appreciate that," Jack replied, walking over to the monitors and watching the images that flashed on the screen. "What's your storage capacity on this feed?"

"Not great, I'm afraid. I usually have two guards in here manning the monitors, one at the front desk, and a few others stationed throughout the building. Inventory is taken on a regular basis, and so far to date, nothing has been reported as stolen or missing."

"Did you have a camera in the Egyptian room during the setup of the exhibition?" Ed asked.

"Yes," Bryce said, reaching for a log book. He skimmed over the page with his finger. "Nothing out of the ordinary was reported. Actually, when I look at this, it appears as if Josh was the only person in the room after midnight."

"Who else was scheduled to work with him?" Ryan asked, coming up behind Bryce to look over his shoulder.

Bryce flipped to a different section of the log. "Jane Ramsey."

"Jane wasn't here last night," Ryan said.

Bryce frowned and flipped another page. "She was here," he insisted.

"Until what time?" Jack asked.

"She signed out at seven-fifteen."

Jack glanced at Ryan. "If you recall, she had mentioned she was here until about seven."

"Yeah, she did. But that would also mean that Josh spent a fair amount of time alone in the room," Ryan said, before looking back to Bryce. "How many people were in the museum after twelve?"

"It looks like just a handful. Three guards, Josh Brody, and the maintenance crew."

"A maintenance crew that didn't open the supply closet," Ed said.

Bryce shrugged. "We have several supply closets located on the premises. It's possible they used the supplies from another."

Ed contemplated his words. "Would it be okay if we took the film? I'd like to have some of our people go over it, to see if they notice anybody unusual or suspicious."

"I'll be happy to make you a copy, but I'm afraid I don't feel comfortable in releasing the original."

"Can you make the copy now?" Ed asked, not willing to take a copy if there was any chance that it wasn't authentic, if there was any chance that it was tampered with.

"Sure. Let me make a quick call," Bryce said, reaching for the cell phone in his pocket. He was only on the phone for a minute. "The guard will be right here to make the copy."

"We appreciate your cooperation," Ed said.

"You can count on my people's full cooperation with everything you need for this investigation," Bryce promised just as the door opened and the guard entered the room. Jack recognized him as Dane Trevor, the same guard who had accompanied Andrew Carstair when he arrived. Bryce took a moment to explain what they needed before he turned back to Jack, Ryan, and Ed. "If you'd like, we can take a tour of the building. I have a pretty good memory of how everything was set up before I left yesterday. Maybe I'll notice something that would suggest what happened last night when Josh died."

"That's a good idea," Ed said.

Bryce nodded. "Then let's go. The copy of the film should be done by the time we return."

Chapter Six

Bright and early the following morning, Jack was at his desk at the police station after a long and sleepless night. The circumstances of Josh Brody's death were weighing heavily on his mind, and he found it difficult to relax at home with so many unanswered questions. He wanted to get some answers that would help put the case to bed.

He sipped his cup of coffee as he thought about the events at the museum the previous evening. There was something that bothered him. Something that he wanted to get a handle on. He didn't like the fact that the body had laid inside a closet all day, without anybody realizing it. That just didn't make sense. At least not with the amount of people that were about. And not with the amount of preparation that should have taken place before the opening of the exhibition. An exhibition that had a lot riding on it. Both in a professional aspect for those involved, as well as monetary for the museum.

Finishing his cup of coffee, he got up from his chair and walked over to the coffee maker in a corner of the room. Refilling his mug with the strong brew, he contemplated on how to proceed. A quick glance at the clock on the wall revealed the time. It was barely six. Too early for Ryan or Ed to make an appearance, but not too early for him to try and get the preliminary results of the autopsy report on Josh Brody.

Walking back to his desk, he took a seat and reached for the phone. After several minutes of conversation with the coroner's office, he placed the receiver back in the cradle and leaned back in his chair, a pensive expression on his face.

"What's the matter?" a familiar voice asked from the doorway.

Jack turned, surprised to find Ryan lounging against the wall. "Hey. You're early. I thought you would want to check on Jane this morning?"

Ryan shrugged. "She was exhausted last night after I dropped her off. I have a feeling she'll spend most of the morning sleeping. So tell me, why are you here so early?" he asked, walking further into the room to help himself to a cup of coffee.

"I couldn't sleep."

"Me neither," Ryan admitted as he leaned back against the counter and looked at Jack from across the room. "What has you so preoccupied? You look like you just received some sort of news."

"I just got off the phone with the coroner's office."

"And?"

"And they completed the autopsy on Brody. They're just waiting for the toxicology results to come in."

Ryan nodded and took a sip from his mug before walking over to his desk and kicking the chair out from under it with his foot. Sitting down, he made himself comfortable. "What are we dealing with?"

Jack leaned back in his chair, swiveling it slightly on its base. "Well for starters, they're estimating Brody's time of death at about two-thirty in the morning yesterday."

"That means that his body would have been in the maintenance closet all through yesterday."

"That's right. Which makes you wonder why, right before an opening of an exhibition, nobody noticed it."

"Bryce Cumming had stated that the maintenance closet is just one of many," Ryan reminded him.

"I know he did. But I don't know if that would really explain how Josh's body remained unnoticed throughout the entire day."

"Unfortunately, we have nothing else to go on right now," Ryan said, taking another sip of his coffee. "What else was the coroner able to tell you?"

"The guy had swelling on the brain due to some sort of trauma."

"Trauma?"

"Yeah."

Ryan's forehead creased in a frown at the news. "But he didn't have any residual bruising visible on his features."

"No, he didn't. Apparently the place of impact was hidden under his hairline."

"Blunt force?"

"Possibly. It could have been caused by a hard fall if his head came into contact with the floor."

"Was there blood present?" Ryan asked, knowing that there was no apparent trace of it in the museum.

"No."

Ryan thought about Jack's words. "Are they contributing his cause of death to the injury?"

"No. They don't think the blow to the head was enough to kill him. Right now they're saying suffocation was the cause of death."

Ryan expelled his breath in a harsh sigh. "That's something I didn't expect."

"I didn't either."

"The closet where we discovered the body has air circulating through," Ryan said, thinking back to the enclosure and the air vent high on one of the interior walls.

"I know. Plus, if you recall, the door doesn't lie flush with the ground. There was about a half-inch opening that would have allowed fresh air to flow through," Jack reminded him.

"Which would lead us to believe that Josh Brody was

already dead when his body was placed in the maintenance closet."

"Everything is pointing in that direction."

"Suffocation would be a pretty easy method of murder to carry out. A plastic bag would be all that was needed."

"I agree. And any evidence of the crime would be easy enough to dispose of. Easy enough to get out of the museum undetected," Jack said, thinking of the search that was continuing at the museum. "They were sorting through the dumpsters in the back of the museum when we left. Maybe we'll get lucky and they'll find something we'll be able to tie to this case."

"Let's hope so, but for now the question remains, who placed Brody's body in that closet?"

"I suppose it's possible that he was murdered in the closet. If he went in the closet to retrieve something, it could just be that somebody cornered him inside," Jack said.

"That might account for the glove we found."

"It might. But it's also possible that the glove ended up in the closet after someone tried to hide the body."

"There's only one problem. The closet's a public domain, and we picked up a lot of prints last night. And even though we haven't gotten the results yet, pinpointing the person responsible for Josh Brody's death isn't going to be an easy task," Ryan pointed out.

"I know."

Ryan leaned back in his chair and stretched his legs

out. "They're reviewing the security tape this morning from the room Josh was working in. Maybe someone did come in to meet him, and it'll show on the tape."

"Bryce Cumming said that he has two guards posted to watch the monitors at all times. One of them should have noticed if that was the case," Jack said.

"It could be that they weren't as observant as they should have been."

Ryan's words gave Jack pause. "Or it's possible that they turned a blind eye to what was going on. Maybe they didn't see anyone that raised their suspicions."

"Meaning this was an inside job."

"It would make sense."

"Yeah, it would."

"I have to tell you, I think we need to do a little further investigation on Bryce Cumming. His relationship with Brody automatically makes him a suspect," Jack said.

"Yeah, but to be honest, it doesn't sound like they had much of a relationship. Or that either man was really interested in pursuing one."

"I agree, that's the impression I received from Bryce also. But we have no knowledge of how Josh reacted to the news that he had a brother."

"Jane always spoke very highly about Josh. She never once mentioned that there might be a potential problem in his life."

"Maybe he was a very private person," Jack suggested. "Maybe he didn't believe in wearing his emotions on his sleeve. And besides, we have no idea of just how close Jane was to the man. Were they strictly business associates, or did they have a friendship where he might have felt comfortable sharing parts of his life? Because if what Bryce said is true, and Josh's ability to obtain the job rested with their blood relationship remaining a secret, I would be very surprised if anybody knew of the circumstances of their family tie."

"Maybe when we search Josh's residence, we'll find some answers," Ryan said.

"Maybe."

Ryan was silent for a brief moment before saying, "It'll be interesting to find out if any of the other employees who were in the museum within the last forty-eight hours had any grudges against the guy. We should be able to make some headway regarding that possibility with the list that Carstair promised."

"We'll head over to the museum later this morning to pick it up. We'll get a warrant before we go just to head off any potential problems."

"From what Carstair and Cumming said last night, we shouldn't have any problems," Ryan reminded him.

"I'd rather be safe than sorry. I don't want to show up and find out that one of them had a change of heart with regards to cooperating with the police."

"We'll need a warrant for Josh's house also."

"That goes without saying."

"How much luck do you think we'll have today in getting answers?"

"If everybody is as cooperative as they appeared last night, we should be fairly successful in at least getting a running jump on solving this case. At the very least,

we'll have a pretty good grasp of just what we're dealing with."

Ryan took another sip of his coffee. "What else did
the coroner's office say?"

"Not much. Like I said, they're waiting for the toxicology reports to come in. They requested a rush, so we
should know something soon."

"Good," Ryan replied, as the sound of someone
clearing their throat alerted him that somebody was
coming.

Jack and Ryan looked up, catching sight of Ed walking in with a box of donuts under his arm, and a file
folder in his hand.

"Morning," Ed murmured.

"Good morning," Jack replied. "It looks like you had
the same idea as Ryan and myself as far as getting an
early start."

"Yeah, but to be honest, it wasn't by choice."

"What do you mean?"

"I got a call this morning from the lab."

"What was it regarding?" Ryan asked.

"The results on the sample they picked up from the
floor outside of the exhibition room."

Jack sat forward. "And?"

"And, the substance on the floor turned out to be
soda."

"We already figured somebody broke the rule about
eating and drinking outside the cafeteria," Ryan said.

"Yeah, but something else showed up that we didn't
count on."

"What?" Jack asked.

"Cyanide."

"What were the levels detected? Did they say?" Jack asked, leaning back in his chair as he considered the evidence.

"High enough to kill someone," Ed confirmed.

Jack looked over at Ryan and Ed. "Last night, Bryce Cumming showed us a restoration room that was on the grounds."

"What's your theory?" Ryan asked.

Jack steepled his hands on his desk as he looked at the two men. "If the museum had the right mix of chemicals present, we may be able to pinpoint if the poison originated from on site. If we can prove that, we could possibly narrow down our list of suspects to the employees and volunteers of the museum who worked within the last forty-eight hours."

"If they had access to the room," Ryan said. "We searched the building yesterday. There were a couple of locked doors that only Bryce had the key to. When I questioned Dane Trevor, he said that access to the rooms was extremely limited. The only other key belongs to the man responsible for their upkeep. And he's on vacation for two weeks."

Jack looked over at him. "Did Dane mention the person's name?"

"Yeah. It was Harold Smith. Since the chemicals located in the room are hazardous, the museum takes strict measures to ensure that nobody can gain access without authorization."

"Somebody else has to have the key besides Bryce Cumming and Harold Smith," Jack pointed out.

"I agree," Ed said. "And the logical choice would be the curator, Andrew Carstair. He would have to have complete access to every room in the place."

"Did Dane mention when Smith left for vacation?" Jack asked.

"A week ago," Ryan replied.

"So, he wasn't working the night of Brody's death," Jack surmised.

"No. Apparently the man went to the Bahamas for a vacation."

Ed's gaze encompassed both men. "His whereabouts should be pretty easy to confirm."

"Yeah, they should," Jack agreed.

Ed picked up a pen and jotted down a note on a piece of paper. "I'll run the trace this morning to see if I can get a confirmation of his location."

Jack nodded. "Sounds good."

Ryan looked at Ed. "Jack talked to the coroner this morning."

"And?"

"They're listing suffocation as the cause of death, but the toxicology reports are still out," Jack told him.

"Lack of oxygen is one of the symptoms of cyanide poisoning," Ed said.

"I know."

"There's a very good possibility that Josh Brody was poisoned," Ed said as he walked over to the coffee maker. Placing the box of donuts on the counter, he took one out. "We're going to need a warrant to search the museum again."

"I'll take care of it," Jack promised.

"Let me know if you need any help on getting a rush placed on the request. I can always call in a few favors."

"It shouldn't be an issue."

Ed nodded. "While you start the ball rolling on that, I'm going to put some pressure on getting the toxicology report," he said, pouring himself a cup of coffee.

"Toxicology reports can take several days to come in," Ryan reminded him.

"Some people owe me a few favors. I'll try and collect on them."

"It would be nice to know exactly what we're dealing with before we head out this morning," Jack said.

"That it would. Give me a little time and I'll see what I can come up with."

Chapter Seven

Two hours later, Ed summoned Jack and Ryan into his office. Motioning for them to have a seat, he picked up a fax that was on his desk.

"I have the preliminary toxicology report," Ed told them.

"And?" Jack prompted.

"And, it's like we expected. Cyanide was present," Ed informed them.

Ryan leaned back in his chair at the news. "At least now we have a general idea of which direction to take the case."

Ed nodded. "I was also able to confirm the whereabouts of Harold Smith. He's staying at a resort in the Bahamas. The manager of the hotel was able to confirm that he's been there for the last week for a family reunion. From all indications, the guy is clean."

"No skeletons lurking?" Jack asked.

"No. We pulled all the transaction records for the guy. There's nothing there. But something else did show."

"What?"

"The search team found the twin glove to the one that you picked up in the supply closet."

"Where did they find it?"

"In the dumpster behind the museum's parking lot."

"Did they do any testing on the gloves?"

"They're doing it now, but they're not picking up much. At least nothing that's going to enable us to get a better handle on the case. The glove is common, and so is the size. And quite frankly, the amount of finger-prints we picked up in the maintenance closet doesn't help. There are just too many. Including one from the doorknob that matched Josh Brody's. Unfortunately, there's no way we're going to be able to narrow down the time that he touched the knob, or when other people went into the closet."

"How long before we have the background reports on the people that worked at the museum within twenty-four hours of Josh Brody's estimated time of death?" Ryan asked.

"I have someone gathering the information now. We'll probably have it sometime this afternoon," Ed said.

Jack nodded. "And Bryce Cumming stated he would deliver his own set of background checks to us today, which will give us the ability to cross-reference for any discrepancies."

"It'll be interesting to see if there are any differences. But to be honest, Bryce Cumming came across as a straightforward man. I would be surprised if the data in the reports didn't corroborate each other," Ryan said.

"I would too," Jack admitted. "But it will at least give us something to work with."

"I have resources available as soon as we need them to comb the records," Ed assured them.

Jack looked over at Ed. "Good. In the meantime, I think we can make some progress with this investigation by searching Josh's residence, and seeing what else we can dig up at the museum. The search warrants aren't going to be a problem to get. They're being worked on right now, and I should have them within an hour. Ryan and I can head out this morning to start the search as soon as I have them in hand."

"I have a better idea. I'll have a different team head back to the museum to do another search, and pick up any other information we may need. You two just concentrate on Josh Brody's residence. We'll cover more ground that way."

"Sounds good," Jack said.

"Then it's settled. Have them forward the warrant for the museum to my office and I'll get some people on it. We'll meet back here this afternoon to go over everything."

"Sure. What time?" Ryan asked.

"Let's say around three. That'll give everybody a chance to do what they need to do. Maybe then we'll have enough information to start forming a theory on exactly what happened to Josh Brody on the night of his death."

Later that morning, Jack pulled his car up to the curb by the small one-story ranch house that Josh Brody owned. Parking the car, he looked out at the manicured grounds, the empty driveway. There was nothing on the property that gave any indication that the man had lived with someone. No toys in the yard, no bikes or other cars in the driveway. "It doesn't look like Josh lived with anybody."

"No, it doesn't," Ryan agreed as his gaze followed Jack's. "I think Jane had mentioned that the guy was a little bit of a loner. He liked to be on his own. Both personally and professionally."

"That might explain the reason he was working at the museum by himself the night of his death."

"Yeah, it might."

"Do you think he requested to work alone that night?"

Ryan lifted one shoulder in a slight shrug. "It would make sense. I would have to check with Jane just to be sure."

"Can you call her now?"

"Let me call her a little later just in case she's still sleeping. I'd rather she be running on all cylinders during the conversation. At least then I won't have any doubts as to whether or not she's leaving out any information."

"It's your call. Hopefully she'll be feeling better today," Jack said, falling silent for a moment before asking, "Are you ready to go in?"

"As ready as I'll ever be," Ryan said, before stepping out into the bright sun. He watched as a group of kids rode by on their bikes. "It looks like a family friendly neighborhood."

"Yeah, it does," Jack agreed. "Which brings us to another point. If the guy was truly a loner, why would he choose this neighborhood to live in?"

Ryan shrugged off the observation. "Just because he's more comfortable with his own company, that doesn't mean that he would want to isolate himself completely from civilization."

"True. But the noise factor alone around here would be enough to drive most people out of their mind. It's barely ten o'clock in the morning, and the kids are already swarming the streets," Jack pointed out, as the sound of young, excited voices filled the air.

Ryan laughed at Jack's words. "It's summer, and school's out. What did you expect?"

"I don't know, but it sure wasn't this."

"Kids are known for their boundless energy."

"I guess."

"You might as well start getting used to it. Pretty soon, you'll have a little one of your own running around."

Jack's expression softened at Ryan's words. "I know."

Ryan grinned. "I never would have taken you for the sentimental type."

"What do you mean?"

"I mean, you practically melt at just the mention of the baby."

Jack shrugged. "I've always liked kids."

"It shows," Ryan said before looking at the numerous people that were outside attending to their lawns. "I think we're going to have quite an audience once the criminalists get here."

Jack followed his gaze. "There are a lot of people about," he acknowledged.

"Yeah, there are. And we both know that police investigations always seem to hold a strong fascination for people. The crowd is already starting to build," Ryan said, gesturing with his head to a small group of people beginning to gather on the front porch of a home across the street.

"As long as nobody interferes with the investigation, people can gawk all they want to."

"Amen to that."

Jack motioned to a van coming down the street. "Here comes the search team now."

"They made good time."

"Come on. Let's get this show on the road," Jack said, turning and walking toward the front door.

An hour later, Jack and Ryan stood in the kitchen of Josh Brody's house, going through boxes full of papers that had rested on top of the refrigerator. The rest of the house had been systematically taken apart, as bags of possible evidence had been removed by the criminalists who were thoroughly searching the place. They stepped back as a uniformed officer removed the computer at a small desk in the breakfast area.

"Careful of the door," Jack warned the officer as the man maneuvered through the swinging door in the small entranceway into the kitchen.

"Got it," the officer mumbled as he elbowed his way through.

Jack glanced at Ryan as he sorted through the store coupons that had been carelessly thrown into one of the boxes they were searching. "Find anything?"

"Just coupons. The guy seemed like the thrifty sort," Ryan said, casting the small pieces of paper off to the side while he continued to search the contents. "How about you? Did you come across anything?"

"I'm not sure," Jack said as he held a piece of paper up to read it.

Ryan paused at the statement. "What do you mean?"

"There's a piece of paper in here with some names written on it, but nothing that indicates the purpose of the list."

"Names?"

"Yeah. Take a look," Jack said, handing the paper to Ryan. "Maybe Jane knows them and mentioned them to you in passing."

Ryan studied the list.

"Well?" Jack prompted after several moments of silence.

"The name Carrie Kendall rings a bell."

"In what respect?"

"I can't be certain, but I think Jane had mentioned that Andrew Carstair's secretary was named Carrie."

"If it turns out that the woman works at the museum as Carstair's secretary, it might be a safe bet to assume that the other people listed on that paper also work at the museum."

"Unless the woman was a personal friend of Josh's."

"That is a possibility."

"Yeah, but regardless of what their association was, we now have a few more names to add to the list of people that we need to investigate."

"Not that it means too much at this point."

"No, I know. Is there anything else in the box?"

Jack pushed the box aside. "No, that looks like the only thing that might be of any relevance."

"There's nothing in here either," Ryan said as he finished looking through his box.

"Other than this list of names, the other stuff in here looks pretty mundane," Jack observed, turning to watch a criminalist dust for fingerprints. "Let's go and check out the rest of the place, and see if anybody else found anything of importance. Maybe we'll luck out and something will surface."

"Sure. Let's go."

Chapter Eight

At precisely three o'clock, Jack and Ryan were back in Ed's office waiting for him to put in an appearance.

Ryan glanced at his watch. "What do you suppose is keeping Ed? I thought he said to meet back here at three o'clock?"

"He did," Jack confirmed. "Maybe he's talking to the crime scene investigative team that was dispatched to the museum. He should be here soon. He's pretty good about not keeping people waiting," he said, shifting on his chair to a more comfortable position. "Did you call Jane?"

"Yeah, as soon as we got back to the station."

"How is she?"

"Better. Much better. I think she's beginning to come to terms with Josh Brody's death. At least she's beginning to accept the fact."

"That's good."

"It's a relief if nothing else."

"What's she doing today?"

Ryan shrugged. "I'm not sure. She mentioned that Ashley had called her earlier though."

"Oh?"

"She wanted Jane to spend the day with her. Maybe have lunch. Jane really appreciated the gesture."

Jack smiled at Ryan's words. "That sounds like something Ashley would do. Did Jane accept the invitation?"

Ryan grimaced. "No, she said she didn't feel up to socializing."

"Well, I'm glad Ashley offered."

"Me too," Ryan said before turning toward the open doorway as the sound of a voice reached him. He gestured in the general direction. "Here comes Ed now."

Ed entered the room, closing the door behind him. "How did it go this morning?" he asked, taking a seat behind his desk.

"Nothing earth shattering showed up at Josh Brody's residence," Jack admitted.

Ed was silent for a moment while he contemplated the words. "It was a long shot that there would be something there that was going to slam dunk this case."

"I know," Jack acknowledged before asking, "What did the search team come up with at the museum?"

Ed leaned back in his chair. "Well, we were able to get access to the restoration room."

"Did Andrew Carstair have the key?" Ryan asked.

"His secretary did," Ed replied.

"What's her name?" Jack asked.

Ed's eyes narrowed slightly at the question. "Carrie Kendall. Why?"

"We found a piece of paper at Brody's residence that contained a list of names. Carrie Kendall's name was on it. Ryan had made a comment that he thought she was Carstair's secretary."

"Well, she is," Ed replied before looking in Ryan's direction. "Do you know this woman?"

"No, not personally," Ryan admitted. "Jane had mentioned the name in passing. And since Carrie isn't that common of a name, it sort of stuck with me."

"Did Jane ever make any reference about the woman? Her personality? Her lifestyle?" Ed asked.

"No. Why?"

Ed shrugged. "Just curious. The woman went out of her way to help us today. She took the criminalists on a guided tour of the facility herself."

"It sounds like she's trying to be accommodating," Jack said.

"It appears that way."

Jack heard just one word. "Appears?"

Ed stared at Jack for a moment before reaching for the files that were laying on his desk. He handed the first one to Jack. "Here's the background check on the woman."

Jack reached for the file and opened it. After skimming through the data, his eyes shot up to meet Ed's. "This report says that Josh and Carrie were often seen together away from the museum, and that their relationship appeared to be more than platonic. From the eyewitness accounts, it seems like they were dating."

"It looks that way."

Ryan reached out to take the file from Jack so that he could look at it. When he was done, he closed the manila folder and placed it back on the desk. "I don't think Jane was aware that Josh Brody was romantically involved with anyone. At least if she was, she never mentioned it."

"Maybe she had no reason to mention it," Jack suggested.

"Maybe," Ryan conceded.

Ed motioned to the file with his chin. "This information targets the woman as a suspect."

"Because she was seeing the guy?" Ryan asked.

"No, because she didn't admit that she was. She gave the officer present at the scene some story about how she only knew Brody in a business sense."

"How did we come up with the information that they were involved together?" Jack asked, wondering why the woman wasn't forthcoming with the information.

"The officer who ran the check was very thorough. He interviewed the superintendent of the woman's apartment, as well as her neighbors. Josh and Carrie saw a lot of each other."

"So the question is, why was she trying to hide her association with the man?" Jack asked.

"Jane had mentioned that the museum's board of directors frowned upon fraternization among fellow employees. That might explain why the woman was holding back information on her involvement with Brody. Maybe she thought it would put her job in jeopardy," Ryan said.

"Possibly," Ed conceded. "But this is something that we're going to have to investigate further. We'll have to bring the woman in for formal questioning. Let her know that we're aware of her relationship with Josh Brody, and see how she reacts to the news."

"You want to blindside her."

"I want to know what happened to Josh Brody. If shocking people into talking is the only way to get answers, I have no problem in following that avenue."

"I agree," Jack injected.

Ed looked at Ryan. "Tell me now if this case is going to be a conflict of interest for you. I know you assured me before that it wasn't, but to be honest, I'm getting a different impression from you."

Ryan met Ed's stare head on. "I told you there wouldn't be a problem. I meant it."

"We can't afford to let personal feelings get in the way of this investigation," Ed said.

"They won't."

Ed nodded. "Then I think we need to come up with a plan to bring the woman in for questioning."

"Let's do it tomorrow," Jack suggested.

"Why not today?"

"Think about it. The woman just gave a statement to the police. She thought she was being accommodating in helping the authorities investigate the museum grounds. If we bring her in today, she'll know something's up. We want her to be calm when she comes in. Not on the defensive."

"I agree with Jack. I think we'll get a more honest response out of the woman tomorrow," Ryan said.

"Okay, that's fine with me," Ed said.

"What else do we know so far?" Jack asked, motioning to the other files on Ed's desk.

"We have a possible explanation of why the maintenance supply closet wasn't used that day. Apparently, the museum received an extra shipment of cleaning supplies and decided to use the excess before storing the remainder in the basement."

"It sounds plausible," Ryan acknowledged.

"We have nothing to refute it," Ed said.

"Do we have anything else?" Jack asked.

Ed shrugged. "There doesn't appear to be any inventory missing, so we can rule out theft as a motive," he said, pushing the files across the desk in their direction. "With regard to any other theory, you'll have to draw your own conclusions. Take a look at what we have to work with."

Jack and Ryan opened the files and began to scan the contents.

Ed gestured to the file that Jack held. "The first page gives a breakdown on the chemicals that are stored at the museum for restoration purposes."

Jack read through the document. "There's nothing here to suggest that the poison originated from the room."

"I know."

"Which means that we might not be able to narrow the search to just the employees of the museum."

"Unfortunately, that's a fact. They did preliminary testing on all the soft drinks stored in the museum's cafeteria. No cyanide was present," Ed revealed.

"And there was only an empty soda case at Josh Brody's residence. There weren't any open or un-opened cans to test," Ryan said.

"There's every possibility that the soda that con-tained the poison might have been a single, isolated case," Ed said.

"Which supports the theory that Josh Brody was the intended target," Jack concluded.

Ryan looked at Ed. "What about the surveillance tapes from the museum? Anything in them?"

Ed shrugged. "We're not sure yet. I have a couple of people scanning them now. They're under strict or-ders to report back to me immediately with anything suspicious."

"Did Carstair give us the list of employees and vol-unteers?" Jack asked, reading through the rest of the file that he held.

"Yeah, and Bryce Cumming sent over copies of his background reports. The file Ryan has contains the background reports our own people were able to obtain up to this point. You two can take the files with you and start sorting through the contents."

"Did you get a chance to look through them?" Ryan asked.

"Briefly."

Jack looked at Ed. "Nothing jumped out at you?"

"Just the report on Carrie Kendall. That's why I isolated it in a different file. But you two are a fresh pair of eyes. Maybe something will click with you. Something that either Jane or your search of Josh Brody's house will bring to light."

"Time will tell," Jack said.

Ed looked at Ryan. "Last chance to back out of the investigation. I'll understand."

"I'm in it for the duration."

"Good. Then I'll leave it to you two to start to sort through this mess."

Chapter Nine

It was after six that evening when Jack parked in his driveway. He was exhausted. The lack of sleep from the night before, as well as the fast pace of the day had left him feeling spent and drained. But even though he was ready to crash, he still had a pile of reports to sort through before he could call it a night.

His thoughts automatically went back to the events of the day. After the meeting with Ed that afternoon, he and Ryan had spent the remaining time at the station reviewing the background reports on the employees and volunteers at the museum, as well as examining footage of the security tapes. They were looking for something, anything that would assist with the investigation of Josh Brody's death. So far, they had come up empty-handed. There was nothing concrete in any of the information uncovered that tied anybody to Josh.

That was with the exception on the possible lead about Carrie Kendall, and the relationship that existed between Josh Brody and Bryce Cumming.

Further investigation into Josh's and Carrie's relationship revealed that the two had gone to great lengths to keep their relationship a secret. Credit card receipts showed a trail of clandestine meetings in out of the way places. Away from familiar faces. It was something that Jack didn't understand. Regardless of the museum's stance against fraternization among its employees and volunteers, he couldn't believe the amount of secrecy involved.

He was deep in thought when a slight movement of the vertical blinds in the bay window in the front of the house caught his attention. He looked up to catch a glimpse of Ashley looking out at him. The sight caused him to smile. He automatically lifted a hand in greeting before reaching for the door handle of the car.

Ashley opened the door and waited in the doorway to the house, watching as he walked up the front walk. "Jack," she greeted with a warm smile.

"Hi, babe," he replied, taking the final steps that brought him within touching distance of her. Leaning down, he pressed a brief kiss to her lips. "Miss me?"

"More than you know."

"I missed you too."

"I'm glad," she teased.

He smiled and reached out to caress her face. "How was your day?"

"Good. And yours?"

"Uneventful," he said, following her into the air-conditioned house. The evening news was playing on the TV, and he paused as his attention was momentarily diverted when a picture of the World Museum flashed on the screen, along with pictures of the police investigation.

Ashley followed his gaze. "The story's been running all day."

Jack grunted. "Figures," he said, shrugging out of his suit jacket.

Ashley reached out to take his jacket, folding it across her arm as she watched him loosen his tie. "I found out some information today that I think you might find interesting."

"What's that?" he asked absently, his attention still on the televised news story.

"I found out that Josh Brody was dating Andrew Carstair's secretary."

Jack froze at hearing her confirm what they had already discovered. He turned to look at her, momentarily stunned by her words. "What?"

Ashley didn't notice his reaction. She was busy hanging up his suit jacket so that she could drop it off at the dry cleaners the following day. "I said, I found out that Josh Brody had been dating Andrew Carstair's secretary."

"How did you find that out?" Jack asked. The information wasn't public knowledge. Of that much he was certain. The trail that they had followed that day to come to the same conclusion had been filled with twists and turns. Only someone who had a vested interest in finding out the truth of the association between Josh Brody and Carrie Kendall would have been able to determine the true nature of their relationship.

"I got a call today from one of the reporters that I used to work with at the paper," she said.

"So?" he asked, not seeing the relevance to her statement. She frequently received calls from her past co-workers.

"So, apparently there was a crew at the museum last night and they saw me there."

"And now they're covering the story on what happened?"

"You got it."

Jack sighed. "They're looking for you to fill in the blanks."

"That's right."

"What did you tell them?"

She shrugged. "Not much. I mean, there's not much to tell at this point."

"Would you tell them if you did know something?" he asked, curious about just how strongly she wanted to get back into reporting, just how much she missed the adrenaline rush that came with covering stories.

"You should know better than to even ask me that," she chided.

Jack smiled at her response. "You're right. So tell me, how did you find out that Josh was seeing Carrie Kendall?"

Ashley walked further into the living room and took

a seat on the sofa. "Amy Redding, the woman who called me, has been covering the society column for the paper for the last six months. When she heard that the Egyptian exhibition was opening, she wanted to write an in-depth article on what it took to set up an exhibition of that magnitude."

Jack sighed at her words. "Let me guess. She took it upon herself to follow Josh Brody."

"Yes. She wanted to do a piece on the life of a designer."

Jack shook his head in confusion at her words. "If that was the case, why would she follow Josh Brody? Jane was the senior designer."

"Well, that's the interesting part. Apparently, Josh was being touted as the true genius behind the exhibition."

Jack was silent for a moment while he digested the information, and the implications behind the remark. Moving over to the sofa, he took a seat next to her. He studied her expression, trying to read the nuances of her body language, of her words. "How trustworthy is Amy Redding?"

"Very."

"Do you believe there was professional rivalry between Jane and Josh?" he asked bluntly, knowing that was where this information was leading to. There was no other explanation of why Ashley would bring it up or why Redding would.

"Amy swears there was. At least by the accounting of the board of directors at the museum."

Jack nodded slightly as he tried to wrap his mind around the information.

"Jack?"

"Yeah?"

"You do realize that if this information proves to be true, Jane is a possible suspect in Josh Brody's murder."

Jack didn't respond to her statement.

"How are we going to tell Ryan?" she asked.

"We're not."

"You can't keep this a secret. He can't find out about it from someone else. It would destroy him."

"We don't have any proof that what Amy said is true."

"She's a reliable source."

"I'm not going to throw this bombshell at Ryan until I have more tangible proof."

"Then I'll get it."

"How?"

"I still have a lot of connections. Tomorrow morning, I'll start making some calls. If there's any truth to it, I'll know."

"And if it's just a rumor? Gossip?"

"We'll just have to consider the source."

Jack reached up to rub the back of his neck wearily. "I don't like you getting involved in this."

Ashley smiled and reached out to squeeze his hand reassuringly. "Relax. I'm not getting involved. Just think of this as doing research."

Jack grasped her hand in his. "Just make sure that nobody knows what you're doing."

"I'll be totally discreet."

"If you think you'll have any luck in getting answers, I would appreciate the help," he conceded.

"I'll get started first thing in the morning."

Jack smiled slightly. "Not first thing. You need your rest."

Ashley rolled her eyes slightly. "I'm pregnant, Jack. Not incapacitated."

"I just don't want you to overdo things."

"I won't," she promised.

Jack stared at her silently for a moment before agreeing. "Okay," he replied, leaning back into the sofa.

Ashley was surprised by the ease in which he agreed, but she didn't want to make a federal case of it. "Okay."

Jack smiled slightly. "Let's give this a rest right now. We have other things to decide."

"Like what?"

"Like what we're going to have for dinner."

"Actually, Italian food sounds good."

"We had Italian the other night."

"I've been craving it."

Jack smiled at her words. "Craving it?"

"Yeah. Lasagna especially."

"Is takeout okay? I need to review some evidence tonight, and sort through some background checks."

"Takeout is fine. And if you need to work tonight, that's okay too. But if that's the case, I'd like to take a ride with you so that we can at least spend some time together."

Jack smiled at her words. "Sure. Why don't you call in the order and then we'll head out."

"Okay. Any preferences for your entrée?"

"Whatever you're having is fine."

Chapter Ten

Later that evening, Jack and Ashley waited for their take-out order in the bar area of Palermo's, a little Italian eatery that was known for its authentic cuisine. The restaurant was crowded, and the waiters bustled around.

"They're busy tonight," Jack observed, glancing impatiently at his watch.

"They warned me on the phone that we might have a little bit of a wait," Ashley said.

Jack looked over at her. "You've been having a lot of cravings lately for Italian food."

She grimaced. "I know. I'll have to be sure that I walk every day in order to keep the weight in check."

"You're eating for two now. I think a healthy appetite is normal."

"We'll know in a week. That's when they're doing the next ultrasound."

"We'll get a chance to hear the heartbeat at that point, won't we?"

"Yes. I can hardly wait," she replied wistfully, her hand automatically going down to protectively lay on her stomach.

Jack's gaze followed the motion. "I already told Ed that I need a couple of hours off that day."

"I'm glad you're coming with me."

"I wouldn't miss it."

Ashley smiled, and her eyes scanned the crowded restaurant. After a long moment, she asked, "Do you see who I see?"

Jack followed her gaze. "Who?"

"Jane."

"Jane and Ryan are here?" he asked, craning his neck to get a better view.

"No. Jane and Andrew Carstair are here."

"Where?"

"At a table on the other side of the room."

Jack glanced around until he caught sight of them. "I wonder what they're doing here?"

Ashley shrugged. "They're good friends. That much I could tell from seeing them at the museum the night that Josh Brody's body was found."

"They look very involved in whatever conversation they're having."

"They work together. I'm sure they have a lot to talk about."

"They seemed to have a lot to discuss the night of Josh Brody's murder," he replied absently.

Ashley watched as Andrew covered Jane's hand with his own. "Should we go over there and say hello?"

Jack turned to look at her. "Yeah, maybe that would be a good idea," he said, thinking it would give him the opportunity to get a better feel for the relationship between Jane and Andrew. A better idea of just what they were discussing.

"Then let's go."

Jack kept his hand protectively on Ashley's lower back as they crossed the room. He watched the deep concentration on Jane's and Andrew's face as they spoke quietly to each other, and he realized that they were so deeply involved in their conversation that they weren't aware that they were about to be interrupted.

"Jane . . ." Ashley began, not waiting to catch their attention before she spoke.

Jane looked up with a slight start. Her eyes flew to both Ashley and Jack. "Hi," she said softly, clearly surprised to see them.

"Hi," Ashley replied. "Jack and I were waiting for a takeout order when we noticed you and Andrew. We wanted to stop by and say hello."

Andrew's eyes met Jane's briefly at Ashley's words. After a moment, he turned to look at Jack and Ashley. "Would you like to join us?"

Jack didn't miss the look that transpired between Andrew and Jane, and he couldn't help but be suspicious of it. Both of them appeared disconcerted by the interruption, and he had a feeling it was due to more than just being caught unaware. There was a definite tension in the air. "Thanks, but no. Like Ashley said, we just wanted to stop by and say hello. We have no intention of intruding on your evening."

"It's no intrusion," Andrew replied.

Ashley thought Andrew's response seemed automatic and a little contrived. He seemed unable to totally mask his relief at Jack's assertion that they weren't planning on staying. Turning to look at Jane, she was slightly surprised to see that the relief was mirrored on Jane's expression. "How are you feeling, Jane?"

"Better, thanks."

"Is Ryan joining you?" Jack asked, curious about how she would react to the question.

"No. I talked to him earlier and asked if he wanted to join us, but he said he had a long day," she said, her eyes not quite meeting his.

"He was down at the station early," Jack admitted, sensing her discomfort with the question.

"I figured he would be."

Andrew looked at Jack. "I turned over all the information the police requested."

"I know. We appreciate your cooperation."

"Do you have any ideas on what happened to Josh?" Jane asked tentatively, almost as if she was afraid to broach the subject.

"Not yet," Jack replied smoothly, not wanting to release any information that the police had been able to uncover.

"I was afraid of that. I was pretty sure Ryan would

have mentioned to me if they had found any leads on the case."

Jack smiled without responding to her comment. Her words gave him pause. Ryan needed to be very careful about what type of information he revealed to Jane. Especially in light of the fact that Jane was a possible suspect in the case, a fact that Jack realized he wouldn't be able to ignore. Though he knew the information might strain the bonds of friendship that he and Ryan had cultivated, he couldn't take a chance that Ryan would have on blinders about Jane. Because the fact of the matter was that regardless of whether or not Jane had anything to do with Josh Brody's death, she might be innocently socializing with the man's murderer.

"I'm sure Ryan will keep you informed of any groundbreaking information," Ashley said.

"I'm sure you're right," Jane replied.

Jack looked at his watch. "We've taken up enough of your time. Our order should be just about ready. We'd better head over to retrieve it."

Andrew smiled. "We appreciate you stopping by."

Jack nodded. Placing his hand on Ashley's back, he prompted her to say her good-byes. "Ash?"

Ashley smiled at Andrew before looking at Jane. "I'm glad we ran into you tonight. Enjoy your evening."

"You too," Jane responded, watching as Jack guided Ashley away from their table.

Ashley waited by Jack's side while he paid for their order. "Don't look now, but I think they're still watching us," she warned.

"I'm sure they are. They looked a little unsettled by our presence here tonight."

"I guess Ryan didn't tell Jane that this is one of our favorite restaurants."

"I guess not."

"So what did you think of their behavior?" she asked as he picked up the bag that contained their dinner and escorted her outside.

Jack waited until they reached the car before he answered. "I'm not sure. Something doesn't seem right to me."

"I know what you mean."

Jack was surprised by her comment. "You changed your mind about nothing going on between the two of them?"

"No. I still don't think there's anything intimate between them."

"But?"

"But, I definitely get the feeling that they're hiding something."

"I agree."

"The question remains though, what?"

"I'm not sure. The only thing I know for certain is that I have to talk to Ryan tomorrow about my suspicions."

"What made you change your mind?" she asked, referring to his statement back at the house about not saying anything until he had something concrete to back his suspicions.

"I can't afford to take any chances that Ryan will say something to Jane about the case, even inadvertently," he said, ushering her into the car before going around to the driver's side. After getting in, he started the engine. "Are you still going to see what you can find out tomorrow about Jane?"

"Of course. Unless you changed your mind . . ."

"No. There's just one thing."

"What?"

"Will you call me on the cell phone if you find out any information while I'm at work?"

"Of course."

"Thanks."

"No problem. Now let's go home. Our dinner is getting cold."

Chapter Eleven

The following morning, Jack was getting ready for work when the phone rang. Placing his razor on the vanity top, he listened as he heard Ashley pick up the receiver from the other room.

"Jack?"

"Yeah?"

"It's Ryan."

"I'll be right there," he promised, picking up a towel to wipe off the shaving cream on his face before walking to the phone. He took the receiver. "Ryan? What's up?"

"Morning, Jack. I was wondering if you would be able to cover for me this morning?"

"Sure. Is everything okay?"

"Yeah. Jane called me this morning. She asked if I would stop by to talk to her before heading to the station."

94   *Cynthia Danielewski*

Jack glanced at the small clock resting by the phone. "It's kind of early. It must be important for her to want to see you."

"Yeah, that's what I thought."

"Well, don't worry about anything. I'll make your excuses to Ed. Just do me a favor, would you?"

"What?"

"Be careful about discussing too much of the case with Jane at this point."

"Don't worry. I know we have to be discreet until we get a better handle on exactly what we're dealing with. I'll meet you down at the station when I'm through. I shouldn't be that long."

"All right. Bye."

Ashley walked up behind Jack, absently drying his shoulders with the towel that was hanging around his neck. "Is Ryan okay?"

Jack turned. Capturing her around the waist, he dropped a light kiss against her lips. "So he says."

"I overheard part of the conversation. Who wanted to see him? Jane?"

"Yeah."

"Maybe she wants to tell him about running into us at the restaurant last night."

"Maybe."

"It would make sense."

"Why's that?"

"I'm sure she wouldn't want Ryan to find out that she was at the restaurant with Andrew Carstair from us."

Jack smiled slightly at her reasoning. "You're forgetting one thing."

"What's that?"

"According to what Jane told us, she invited Ryan to go with them last night," he said, reminding her of Jane's remark from the night before.

"So she says."

Jack was surprised by Ashley's comment. "Don't tell me that you think she was lying?"

"Lying, no. But I don't think she was entirely truthful with Ryan about the purpose of her meeting with Andrew. She was just a little too uncomfortable with our presence at the restaurant."

"So you believe she wants the opportunity to talk to Ryan about last night before we do."

"Exactly."

Jack was silent for a moment before conceding, "You may be right."

"I would bet money on it."

"I guess I'll find out later on this morning when I see Ryan."

"I suppose," Ashley agreed before changing the subject. "Why don't you finish shaving, and I'll go and make breakfast."

Jack grimaced. "I'm not hungry."

"But I am."

"So?"

"So, I don't feel like eating alone. And you're supposed to cater to pregnant women."

"You are?"

"Yes. I have it on good authority."

"Well, far be it from me to break tradition."

"I was hoping you would say that," she said, reaching up to absently brush a stray lock of hair off his forehead. "Why don't you finish getting ready. I'll see you downstairs when you're done."

"Okay."

Fifteen minutes later, Jack entered the kitchen, his suit jacket hooked over his shoulder. "Something smells good," he said, walking up behind her to glance over her shoulder. "Something besides you, that is."

Ashley laughed. "Flattery will get you everywhere."

"I was counting on it," he said, dropping a light kiss on her nape before walking over to fold his suit jacket over a chair. Reaching out, he picked up a coffee mug and headed to the coffee maker.

Ashley looked up from beating the egg mixture for the French toast she was making. "Are you going to tell Ryan about Jane when you see him?"

Jack took a sip of his coffee before kicking a chair out with his foot to take a seat at the table. "I guess that depends on what he says to me."

"What do you mean?"

"I mean, I want to feel him out first. I want to find out just what the reason was for Jane wanting to see him this morning."

Ashley considered his words as she dipped the first

slice of French bread into the egg mixture. "I guess that makes sense."

"I suppose you would come out and tell him right away?" he asked.

"No. Theoretically it makes sense to see what Ryan says first. I don't want us to be responsible for any problems between Jane and Ryan. Especially if it turns out that her meeting with Andrew last night was innocent," she conceded, removing two slices of French toast from the frying pan and placing them on a plate.

Jack reached for the syrup as soon as she placed the plate in front of him. "I'm glad you're thinking rationally."

"I just don't want Ryan hurt."

"Neither do I. And that's the reason we have to be careful in how we approach him with this."

Ashley took a seat across from him with her own breakfast. "I'll call you if I find out anything today."

"Okay," Jack replied, taking a bite of his French toast.

Ashley watched him eat. "How is it?"

"It's good."

"I'm glad you like it. I tried a new recipe."

Jack took another bite, trying to taste the ingredients she used. "Cinnamon and vanilla?"

"Yes. One of the ladies at my doctor's office gave me the recipe. She said she used to crave French toast when she was pregnant with her first child."

"Well, you have to admit, it's better than craving Italian food first thing in the morning."

Ashley grimaced. "That craving usually doesn't hit until about noon."

"Why don't you make a lasagna today and freeze individual portions for yourself so that you'll have it when the craving hits?"

"That's not a bad idea. But I don't know if I'll have time to do it today," she said, finishing the last of her French toast before picking up her cup of decaffeinated coffee to take a sip.

"Why's that?"

"I wanted to go to the library to see what articles I can find on the World Museum and its opening."

"The place hasn't been open that long. I'm sure you already read all the articles that were written up on the place."

"True," she acknowledged. "But I didn't pay that much attention to them when they originally ran."

"Your memory is pretty good."

"Yes, but I think I recall a few pieces on Andrew Carstair that I didn't really pay attention to. I'm hoping there might be something there that might shed some light on the man."

"You need to be careful on just how involved you get in this case," Jack cautioned.

"I'll be very careful. Just what could happen at a library anyway?"

"Nothing, I suppose. But don't let anyone know why you're researching the man and the museum. We have a killer out there that went to great lengths to commit a crime that couldn't be easily traced. I don't want you to make anyone nervous. It might put you in jeopardy."

"Relax, Jack. I'll take the utmost care to make sure that nobody knows what I'm doing and why."

At her words, Jack leaned back in his chair and studied her across the table. "Other than the library, were you planning on going anywhere else?"

"Not that I know of. Why?"

"No reason. I just don't want to be worrying about you today."

Ashley smiled at his words. "Relax. I'm not planning on doing anything that will put our baby in jeopardy."

"Or yourself?"

"Or myself."

Jack relaxed slightly at her words. "Okay."

"You worry too much."

"I prefer to think of it as being cautious."

"Semantics."

"No, common sense."

"Everything will be fine."

Jack stared at her silently before saying, "I trust that you'll do the right thing."

"Good."

Chapter Twelve

It was close to eight in the morning when Jack arrived at the station. Making his way to his desk, he threw his keys carelessly on the surface before heading over to the coffeepot to pour a mug of the fresh brew. He caught a glimpse of Ed as he walked by his office, and lifted a hand briefly in greeting.

"Jack?" Ed called.

"I'll be right there," Jack replied, quickly fixing his beverage and heading into Ed's office.

Ed motioned to a chair in front of his desk. "Take a seat."

"Sure."

Ed leaned back in his chair, causing the springs to creak under his weight. "Where's Ryan?"

"He went to see Jane."

"Everything okay?"

100

Jack shrugged. "I'm not sure. She called him this morning and wanted to see him before he came to the office. I told him I would cover for him until he got here."

Ed nodded. "I spoke to Carrie Kendall last night."

"And?"

"And she asked if she could come in this morning at eight-thirty. Apparently she has to be at the museum by ten, and she didn't want to take time off work to come down to meet with us."

"I take it you told her that was okay."

"Yes. Do you think you can handle the interview on your own? I have a meeting at nine with the district attorney."

"Sure, not a problem."

"Good. Just remember, we need to see if we can get her to talk to you about her relationship with Josh Brody."

"You got it."

"Then I'll leave her in your capable hands."

Jack nodded. "Anything else?"

"No, that was it."

Jack rose from his chair and stretched his legs. "Then I'm going to go and get caught up on some paperwork while I wait for her."

"Okay."

Jack was at his desk working on a report when his intercom buzzed. "Reeves," he said, listening as the front desk announced that Carrie Kendall was waiting for him. After instructing the desk sergeant to show her into an interrogation room, he stood up and headed for the door.

Jack caught a glimpse of Carrie as he walked toward the room she was waiting in, and he was surprised by her appearance. She was nothing like he expected. He usually associated people working in a museum as professional in nature, polished in much the same way as Jane. But Carrie Kendall's demeanor threw him. She resembled a bohemian. Literally. Long blond hair parted down the middle flowed to her waist, and a prairie-style skirt and top completed her ensemble. There was no polish on her nails, no makeup graced her features. She looked like the type of person that was entirely comfortable in her own skin. Entirely comfortable with nature.

He kept his expression neutral as he walked toward her. Stretching out a hand in greeting, he said, "Carrie Kendall?"

A pair of vivid blue eyes met his. "Yes. And you are?"

"Detective Jack Reeves."

Her eyes briefly skimmed over him. "It's a pleasure to meet you."

"And you," he returned, gesturing to the small table surrounded by chairs. "Please, take a seat."

"Thank you." She watched covertly as he closed the door, shutting out the voices of the other people walking by. "I appreciate you taking the time to meet with me so early."

Jack shrugged. "I appreciate you taking the time to meet with us."

"It's not a problem. I understand from Captain Stall that you had some questions for me?"

"Yes," Jack said, pulling out a chair to take a seat.

"Regarding Josh Brody?"

Jack's eyes met hers. "Yes," he confirmed, studying her actions, watching her behavior. She looked perfectly calm. There was nothing in her body language or her tone of voice that hinted at any sense of unease that she may have been feeling at meeting with him one on one. That surprised him. Usually, just the thought of meeting with the police was enough to make anybody nervous. But she appeared cool and in control. Which wasn't what he expected. Her demeanor was totally at odds with someone who had gone to great lengths to keep a relationship secret.

"I'll help in any way I can."

"I appreciate that. Because the reason we wanted to meet with you was because we found out about your relationship with Josh Brody," he said simply, bluntly.

"What?"

Jack noticed the way she stilled at his words. It was only for the briefest of moments, but it was noticeable. He leaned forward in his chair, studying her across the table. "We found out about your relationship with Josh Brody," he repeated.

"I see," she murmured softly.

"We also found out about the lengths the two of you

went to in order to keep the relationship a secret. I need to know why you felt it was necessary to do that."

She didn't say anything at first, she just continued to stare at him, gathering her thoughts.

"Miss Kendall?"

The mention of her name broke the trance she had succumbed to. "I'm not ignoring you. I'm just thinking of the best place to start."

"The beginning is always good," he encouraged softly.

She nodded. Taking a deep breath, she removed her hands from the table and folded them in her lap. "I met Josh the first day I started working at the museum."

"And?" he prompted once more when it didn't look like she was going to say anything else. He studied her silently, noticing the way she had removed her hands from the table. He had a feeling she did that because she was nervous. Disconcerted in a way that she didn't want to show.

"And, he was charming. A little offbeat, a little stringent in his work ethic, but definitely charming," she said, her voice softening as she recalled the man.

"What do you mean by offbeat?"

"Josh was a multitude of contradictions. He was a perfectionist in his work by anybody's standards, but he wasn't as uncompromising in other areas."

"Such as?"

"Such as following policy and regulations."

"Meaning?"

"Meaning, if there was a rule to be broken, Josh usually broke it. If somebody told him not to do something, he usually went out of his way to do it."

"Just to prove that he could," Jack said, realizing that the woman just gave him an insight into Josh's character.

"That's right."

Jack relaxed slightly in his chair, his body language inviting her to do the same. He wanted to keep her talking. He wanted to find out just what else she would reveal about Josh Brody. "What kind of rules did he break?"

"Little things. Drinking soda outside the cafeteria, seeing me outside business hours, breaking with convention when it came to setting up the displays," she replied, her words drifting off.

Jack noticed the glimmer of tears in her eyes as she recalled Josh, and he steeled himself against offering any sympathy. He wanted her to talk. To open up. He didn't want to distract her in any way. "You mentioned his drinking soda outside the cafeteria," he said, thinking about the report that came back on the soda found on the floor. Her words pretty much confirmed that the drink belonged to Josh Brody, which meant that the theory held up about the man being dead before his body was placed in the closet.

"I know that sounds like a pretty silly rule to break considering the amount of money the artifacts at the museum are worth," she conceded.

"It does kind of go against the perfectionist image. Taking a chance on spilling something on valuable museum pieces seems a little careless."

"Josh was always very careful."

Jack didn't want to debate a point that would accomplish nothing. "Would you have any idea of why he felt the necessity to break the rules that the museum had set up?"

She was quiet for a moment before admitting, "I think it was because of his problems with Andrew Carstair."

Jack stilled at her words. "Problems?"

"Yes. I don't know if you're aware of this, but Josh actually applied for Jane Ramsey's position at the museum."

"He has the experience for the job?"

"Yes. But he missed out on getting the position due to politics."

"What do you mean by that?"

"I mean that Jane Ramsey had a history with Andrew Carstair. They had worked together in the past, and they seemed to get along well. Personally, I don't think Jane had any more experience than Josh for the job."

Jack frowned. "And you're basing that assumption on . . ."

"I'm basing it on the records that are kept in Andrew Carstair's office."

"Which you have access to," Jack concluded.

"That's correct."

"Was there any animosity between Josh Brody and Jane Ramsey that you could detect? Any professional jealousy?"

"Not with Josh and Jane."

The way she made the statement had Jack looking at her curiously. "But there was between somebody," he guessed.

"Yes."

"Who?" Jack asked when she didn't elaborate.

"Andrew. He hated Josh."

Chapter Thirteen

"Andrew Carstair hated Josh Brody?" Jack asked, wanting to make sure that he didn't misinterpret her words, her meaning.

"Yes, he did."

"Why?"

"I'm not sure. I think it has something to do with the fact that they used to work together at another museum. But to be honest, I'm not positive. The tension between the two of them was always thick enough to cut with a knife, and I never felt comfortable enough in broaching the subject of why there was so much tangible animosity between them."

Jack drummed his fingers on the top of the table as he considered her words. If what she said was true, he had to wonder why nobody else who worked at the museum mentioned the fact when they were being interviewed. Jack knew that one of the first questions asked of everybody was if they were aware of anybody who might have held a grudge against Josh Brody. If there were any enemies they were aware of. Nobody claimed to know of any. "Let me ask you something."

"Sure."

"How long have you worked for Andrew Carstair?"

"Not long. A little over three months."

"How close are you to him?"

She shrugged slightly. "I work for the man," she responded, skirting the question with a vague answer.

"I need you to be a little more precise."

There was a long pause of silence while she thought about his words. "I'm not sure what you want me to say," she finally admitted.

"Does Andrew take you into his confidence? Did he ever willingly express any discord with Josh Brody?"

"He didn't have to. I could detect it every time Josh came into Andrew's office."

"Which was frequently?"

"I would say about three times a week."

"Under what guise did he come to see Andrew under?"

"Guise?"

"For what reason," he clarified, watching her closely. He couldn't detect anything in her demeanor or voice that would indicate she wasn't being entirely truthful, but he also found it hard to believe that nobody else would have realized that Andrew and Josh had problems with one another.

"Their meetings were strictly business."

"And you're sure about that?"

"Positive. It was all relating to the exhibitions."

"Was Jane Ramsey present during the meetings?"

"A few times. Not always."

"Was Jane aware of Andrew's feelings toward Josh?"

Carrie laughed, but it was without humor. "I fail to see how she couldn't be aware of them."

"You had mentioned that you believe their problems started when they worked together at another museum. Josh never mentioned to you where it was? The location? What capacity they worked together?"

"No. The only thing he let slip one time was that the museum was located in Manhattan."

"Manhattan's full of museums."

"I know."

Jack didn't press her any more on the subject. He knew he would be able to obtain the information through a detailed background report on the two men. Something that was already in the process of being worked on. He abruptly changed the subject. "You never fully explained the reason you and Josh kept your relationship a secret."

"Didn't I?"

"No."

She shrugged apologetically at the oversight. "Sorry, I thought it was obvious. Andrew would have fired me in a heartbeat if he knew I was seeing one of his enemies."

Jack was a little startled by the way she categorized

Andrew's and Josh's relationship. "Enemies is a strong word," Jack pointed out.

"But appropriate."

Jack inclined his head, realizing that she wasn't going to change her perception of the relationship between the two men. "Well, I appreciate you taking the time to come and talk to me."

She waved aside his thanks. "It's not a problem. I want to help find Josh's killer any way I can."

"I appreciate that," Jack said, reaching inside his pocket for a business card. He held it out to her. "Here's my card. Please call me if you can think of anything that you feel might be pertinent to the case."

"I'll do that," she said, placing the card in her purse.

Jack stood. "Would it be all right if I call you if I have any more questions?"

"Of course."

"Thanks. Let me walk you to your car," he said, escorting her from the room.

Five minutes later, Jack was back at his desk, contemplating the information he had learned. He was deep in thought when the sound of footsteps invaded his subconscious. He looked up to find Ryan entering the room.

"Hey," Ryan said.

"Hi."

Ryan walked over to the coffeepot. Pouring a mug full, he glanced at Jack. "Did I miss anything?"

"As a matter of fact, yes."

"What?" Ryan asked, taking his cup and walking over to his desk.

"Carrie Kendall was here."

Ryan glanced at his watch. "So early?"

"She spoke to Ed yesterday and asked if she could come in this morning. She didn't want to take time off work to come down later."

"She sounds conscientious."

"I guess that's a matter of opinion."

"What's she like?" Ryan asked, taking a sip of his coffee.

"Unconventional."

Ryan smiled slightly at the description. "Sounds like my kind of person."

Jack grunted. "She definitely walks to a different beat."

"Nothing wrong with that."

"No."

"Did she say anything?"

"She claims that there was animosity between Andrew Carstair and Josh Brody."

"Interesting."

"Why's that?"

"Because that's exactly what Jane told me this morning."

"Did she?"

"Yes."

"Did she mention anything else to you?" Jack asked.

"She told me she saw you and Ashley last night.

That's the main reason she wanted to see me this morning. She wanted to fill me in with what had happened before I saw you. I think she believes that you and Ashley might think there's something more to her relationship with Andrew Carstair than just business."

"Is there?" Jack asked bluntly.

Ryan gave a short bark of laughter. "No. Their relationship is strictly professional."

"They seem close," Jack said, trying to feel his way around the conversation, not wanting to say anything out of line.

"They are. But it's business."

Jack nodded, not saying anything to question Ryan's belief. "Did you know that she was having dinner with Andrew Carstair last night?"

"Yes, she told me. She asked if I wanted to come, but I didn't want to play third wheel. Especially since the dinner had to do with business at the museum."

Jack reached for his own mug of coffee and emptied it in one swallow. "You said Jane mentioned that Andrew and Josh shared some animosity."

"That's right."

"Did she expand on that?"

"No, but she said that was one of the things Andrew was worried about last night. That we would become suspicious of him based on his feelings toward Josh. I get the feeling that Andrew was trying to set up Jane as a defense against the police last night."

"And was that what Jane thought?"

"Yeah, she did. Which I guess was why she became

concerned about seeing you and Ashley at the restaurant."

"Does Jane know where the bad blood came from between the two of them?"

"Andrew and Josh worked together at the Americana Museum in the city, and the museum had a problem with theft. Josh was the designer of one of the exhibits where several priceless artifacts disappeared. Andrew Carstair was the assistant curator. Both men fell under suspicion during the investigation."

"Were either of the men guilty?" Jack asked, more for clarification sake than anything else. He knew both men would have had to have been cleared. There was no other way they would have been able to stay within the industry. No other way that they would be trusted with the artifacts that were in their care.

"No. It turned out to be one of the security specialists that were on staff. But there was enough mud slinging where some of it stuck. And I guess the hard feelings that they had for one another during that time never disappeared."

"Carrie Kendall seems to think that Josh was just as qualified for Jane's position as Jane."

"He was. Jane confirmed that."

"But she wasn't threatened by him in any way?"

Ryan shook his head. "No. She was happy to have someone she could trust work with her on the exhibit."

"Makes sense."

"You know what I think we should do?"

"What?"

"Head over to the Americana Museum in Manhattan and see if we can find out any information on Josh and Andrew."

"I'm game if you are," Jack assured him.

"And on the way back, I think we should pay another visit to Bryce Cumming."

"I think that's a good idea. You have to wonder why he failed to mention that there were possible problems between Josh and Andrew, especially considering the fact that the problems can be directly traced back to a security breach. Regardless of whether they can be connected to the theft, the fact that they were even under suspicion would carry some weight."

Ryan laughed slightly at Jack's remark. "What happened to the assumption of innocence?"

"I don't think that applies when the stakes are high. The museum shouldn't have been willing to take any risks when it came to protecting its inventory."

"I agree," Ryan said. "So why don't we head out and see what we can find."

Chapter Fourteen

An hour later, Jack drove into a parking garage next to the Americana Museum. Flashing his badge to the guard at the booth, he was able to park the car with minimum effort.

Ryan released his seat belt the moment the car came to a complete stop. "Do you think we should have gotten a warrant before heading over here?"

Jack looked at him. "On what grounds? There's nothing that ties Josh Brody's death to the crime that took place here. Especially considering that the man was exonerated. Right now, we're just looking for information. I think we'd have everybody's antenna going up if we started pulling out the heavy artillery at this point. And quite frankly, I'm not sure if a judge would grant the request until we have something concrete to tie this all together."

"It would probably be a long shot obtaining the warrant."

"Without a doubt. And besides, I don't think we should be tipping our hand at this point. If word of our visit got back to Andrew Carstair, the man might panic. I don't want to scare him off. We're here because we don't have enough evidence to either pinpoint him as a suspect, or exonerate him."

"Yeah, I know. Right now, we seem to have a couple of possible suspects. It's just that Carstair seems to be heading the list."

"But we can't discount Carrie Kendall or Bryce Cumming. Both had an acknowledged relationship with Josh, regardless of the circumstances surrounding their association with the man."

"But did they both have access to the poison that ultimately killed the man?"

"You and I both know that with the right type of incentive and ingenuity, people can pretty much gain access to whatever they want."

"I admit that both Cumming and Carstair would have had the knowledge of where to obtain the poison. But Kendall?"

"I'm not saying she had anything to do with Brody's murder, but we have no evidence that exonerates her. Until something shows indicating she's in the clear, she has to remain on the suspect list."

"I know," Ryan acknowledged. "But it would seem more likely that Carstair or Cumming would know exactly how large of a dose of cyanide would have been necessary to cause Josh's death. Their background alone would give them the basics. In Andrew's position, he has to have a general knowledge of chemical compounds, and Bryce could have probably obtained it from any one of his numerous contacts."

"Granted."

"We also have to keep in mind that Bryce gave no clues that he had bad feelings toward Josh. He was very forthcoming about the relationship as soon as he saw us."

"But he did hide it from everyone else," Jack reminded him.

"He said he had reasons for that."

"Maybe. But the jury is still out with regards to whether or not they were valid reasons."

Ryan nodded and glanced at his watch. "It's getting close to lunch time. I guess we should be heading inside if we want to catch the security director before he heads out for a bite to eat."

"Yeah, let's go," Jack said, stepping from the car. He waited for Ryan to join him before they headed toward the glass doors that led to the museum from the parking garage.

The Americana Museum was bustling with activity as groups of children waited impatiently in the lobby for their tour guides. Jack and Ryan made their way through the crowd, noticing the different displays of artifacts and history.

Jack stopped by the information desk and smiled at the white-haired elderly woman who stood behind the desk. Taking out his badge, he identified himself. "I'm Detective Jack Reeves, and this is Detective Parks. We'd like to talk to the director of security if he's available."

The woman, whose badge read Elaine Cantor, peered at them curiously through her glasses. "That would be Ken Light."

Jack smiled at her. "Is he available?"

"He's in today, but I'm not sure if he's in his office. Let me call him to check," she offered.

"I would appreciate that."

After a few moments, she put the phone back in its cradle. He waited patiently for her to speak.

"Mr. Light would be happy to meet with you," she said, passing over two visitor badges, and pushing a sign-in book in their direction. "If you would both sign in," she requested.

They signed and clipped the badges to themselves.

"Thank you, Ms. Cantor," Jack said.

She nodded. "Mr. Light's office is upstairs. Go down the left corridor to the end, and take the elevator up. It's right by the paleontology exhibit. You can't miss it."

"Thanks," Jack said, turning to walk.

"This place is pretty big," Ryan said, as they passed a wing dedicated to space exploration before they noticed the dinosaur exhibit.

"Bigger than I expected."

"It looks like it's a favorite with kids."

Jack smiled, hearing the excited voices of children as they explored a space capsule. "Yeah, it does."

Ryan motioned ahead. "There's the elevator."

The moment they reached the elevator, Jack pressed the call button. "At least the man is willing to talk to us."

"Yeah. But it remains to be seen what exactly he has to say."

"Nothing ventured, nothing gained."

"Very true," Ryan agreed, as the elevator opened before them. "Let's go."

The moment the elevator door opened on the second floor, a man stepped forward to meet them.

"Detectives? I'm Ken Light," the man said introducing himself. "I understand that you wanted to see me?"

"Mr. Light," Jack said, stretching out a hand to introduce himself. "I'm Detective Reeves and this is Detective Parks. We were wondering if you could spare a few moments. We have some questions regarding a case we're investigating."

Ken Light's eyebrows rose slightly at Jack's words, and he looked at both Jack and Ryan with interest. "Of course. Please follow me. We'll go into my office where we'll have some privacy."

Jack and Ryan followed the man into his office and both looked around curiously at the TV monitors that lined one wall.

"This looks like an impressive security system," Ryan said, automatically scanning the monitors, watching as practically every angle of the museum was videotaped.

Ken smiled slightly. "The one thing that the museum doesn't quibble with is security," he said before motioning to the two chairs in front of his desk. "Please have a seat."

"Thanks," Jack said, folding himself into the chair.

Ken took his own seat. Sitting forward, he steepled his hands. "So tell me, what can I help you with?"

"I don't know if you heard that there was a murder at the World Museum on Long Island," Jack began, watching the man closely, trying to read his facial expression, his thoughts.

Ken frowned. "Yes, I did. It was Josh Brody, wasn't it?"

"Did you know Josh?" Ryan asked.

"Not personally," Ken admitted. "But I know he used to work here."

"That's what we were told," Jack said. "We were hoping you would be able to tell us a little bit about the incident that occurred when Brody worked here."

Ken looked at Jack for a moment before saying, "I would be happy to, but I think you should be aware that you're the second person today that asked for information about that time."

Jack's eyes narrowed. "Who else was looking for information?"

"Bryce Cumming."

Chapter Fifteen

"Bryce Cumming was here?" Jack asked.

"Yes. He was here asking questions about Josh and Andrew Carstair," Ken replied.

"Do you know Andrew Carstair?" Ryan asked.

Ken shook his head. "No, unfortunately, they were both employed at the museum before my time. But after Bryce Cumming started asking questions, I took it upon myself to do a little research on the two," he said, pushing his chair back from his desk and rising. Walking over to an assortment of filing cabinets in the corner, he opened the top drawer and removed several files. He walked back to the desk and handed the documents over. "This is what I have on the two men."

Jack reached for the files. "Thanks."

Ken shrugged and resumed his seat. "Basically, the

only things in there are public records. Nothing earth shattering."

"What about the files from when Josh and Carstair worked here? Where are they?" Ryan asked.

"Archived," Ken replied.

Jack motioned to the documents in his hand. "But not these?"

"No. If you look through those, there are photos of the museum's special events, and the employees and volunteers who were present at the time. We keep those around for posterity's sake more than anything else."

"What do you mean by that?" Jack asked.

Ken shrugged. "Retirement parties, celebrations. Anything along that nature."

Jack scanned through the contents of the first file. "Did you show these to Bryce Cumming?"

"I did. The man seemed genuinely concerned about Josh Brody's employment here at the museum, and there's nothing in those files that's confidential," Ken said.

"Do you have a color copier?" Ryan asked.

"Yes. Why? Did you want to make copies of the photos?"

"If you wouldn't mind."

"Of course not. Though I can't guarantee how clear the photos will come out."

"It will give us a reference point."

"The copier's down the hall. You can help yourself when we're through."

"Thanks."

Jack finished glancing through the files and handed them to Ryan. "So what did you talk about with Bryce Cumming?"

"Nothing really. I couldn't tell him much. But he was asking the same questions that you two gentlemen are."

"Did you know about the theft where Carstair and Brody fell under suspicion?" Ryan asked.

"I did. I couldn't help but be aware of it. It was major news."

"Something was stolen, wasn't it?" Jack asked.

"Yes, some artifacts from the Native American exhibit. They were later recovered by the police. The security specialist who stole them was trying to pawn them on the black market."

"I imagine a lot of people would pay top dollar to have original artifacts in their private collection," Jack said.

"You got that right."

"What was the security specialist's name?" Ryan asked as he finished glancing through the files.

"Gail Barret."

"It was a woman?" Jack asked.

"Yeah, and one of the least likely people that would be suspected."

Jack frowned at the choice of words. "I thought you weren't here at the time the crime took place."

"I wasn't. But I did know Gail."

"Personally?" Ryan asked.

"I knew her from a week-long seminar on museum security."

"What exactly was her job?" Jack asked, surprised by the comment but careful to keep it from showing.

"She was technically a specialist in her field. She was trained specifically to work in high-risk areas. To recognize possible security breaches. Her job was to eliminate the risk to the museum. To keep our insurance premiums low."

"Sounds like a big job for one person," Ryan said.

"Gail was well compensated."

"And well trusted?"

"That's right. She knew all the ins and outs of surveillance. She knew exactly when to make her move, and how to make it so that any hint of guilt wouldn't point in her direction."

"How long was she employed by the museum before she made her move?" Jack asked.

"About a year. Long enough to gain the trust of her co-workers."

"And as far as you know, there was nothing in her history that would have tipped anyone off with regards to what she was planning to do?" Ryan asked.

"Absolutely not," Ken replied without hesitation. "Gail always gave the impression of being very responsible, very professional. Conservative is a good word that comes to mind."

"Evidence of the crime pointed to Carstair and Brody, didn't it?" Jack asked.

"Yes, it did. That goes to show how methodical Gail was. She almost committed the perfect crime."

"Do you know what actually tipped the authorities to look in her direction?" Ryan asked.

"She slipped up. The person that she tried to fence the relics to was an undercover cop."

"If she was as good as she thought she was, she would have known that there was a sting in place," Ryan said.

"She got sloppy. And she's paying for it. Right now, she's serving time upstate."

"And after she was caught, Carstair and Brody found it necessary to leave," Jack deduced.

"From my understanding, they came under a lot of scrutiny during the investigation. Josh was in charge of the exhibition that the artifacts disappeared from, and Andrew Carstair was assistant curator of the museum."

"What about the curator? Why wasn't he under suspicion?" Ryan asked.

"He was out on the family leave act. A member of his family was very ill."

"So basically, Carstair was in charge," Jack said.

"That's right. And something like that happening on your watch is very hard to overcome."

"And since Josh was in charge of the exhibition, it would stand to reason that Andrew would have had a lot of resentment toward the man. Maybe even blamed him for not realizing something was up," Jack remarked.

"It's understandable, and unfortunately things escalated even more after Gail was caught," Ken said.

"What do you mean?" Jack asked.

"Well, she basically tried to implicate Josh in the mess."

"How?"

"She told the authorities that Josh was the one who asked her to try and fence the pieces she took."

"Why would she do that?" Ryan asked.

"Because of their relationship. They were distant cousins."

Chapter Sixteen

Twenty minutes later, Jack and Ryan were heading back toward Long Island, maneuvering through the city traffic. Jack swerved to avoid a cab that had crossed into his lane, and he cursed under his breath at the driver's carelessness.

"Relax," Ryan said.

Jack grunted. "So what did you think about Ken Light?" he asked as he quickly shifted lanes.

Ryan shrugged. "He seemed okay. We'll have to subpoena for Josh Brody's and Andrew Carstair's records after what he told us though."

"Yeah, I know. The man left more questions open than he answered. But at least now we know that there was a definite tie between Brody and the incident."

"It might be all circumstantial."

"It still leaves a lot of unanswered questions."

"Yeah, it does. Like why Gail Barret tried to frame Josh," Ryan said, glancing at his watch. "We should be at the World Museum within thirty minutes. Did you want me to call and let Bryce know we're coming?"

"Do you think that's a good idea?"

"I don't know. It would at least guarantee that the man will be around when we arrive."

"Sure. Go ahead and make the call."

Ryan reached for his cell phone and dialed the number. After a minute of conversation, he disconnected the call. "He'll be waiting for us."

Jack nodded. "What was his demeanor like on the phone? Was he surprised to hear from you?"

"No. He seemed to be expecting the call."

"Nobody can say the man's a fool."

"The man said he'd wait as long as he needed to."

Thirty minutes later, Jack parked in the near-empty parking lot of the World Museum. No people mulled around the front entrance of the museum.

"It doesn't look like they're open," Jack observed.

"No, it doesn't," Ryan said, unbuckling his seat belt.

"Did Jane mention anything about the museum remaining closed for awhile?" Jack asked.

"No, not a thing. It will be interesting to find out what's going on," Ryan said, reaching for his door handle and stepping out of the car into the hot summer sun.

Jack did the same. "Yeah, it will. Come on. Let's go."

Walking toward the front door, they noticed a security guard standing watch. Jack recognized him from the night that Brody's body was found. It was Dane Trevor.

Jack nodded in greeting before asking, "Is the museum closed?"

"Locked up tighter than a drum," Dane replied.

"Under whose orders?" Ryan asked.

"It was a mutual decision between Andrew Carstair and Bryce Cumming. They don't want to take any chances on contaminating any evidence that would help with Josh Brody's murder investigation."

Jack's eyebrow rose at the news. "That's very conscientious of them," he said, knowing that the crime scene had been released.

Dane shrugged. "Everybody is very concerned about what happened to Josh."

Ryan glanced around the nearly empty corridor. With the exception of a few people walking through the hallway, the place was practically deserted. "How long are they closing down for?"

"Until further notice I'm told," Dane said.

Ryan nodded. "Is Bryce Cumming in his office?"

"Yes. He's expecting you."

"Thanks," Ryan replied before turning to Jack. "Ready?"

"I'm right behind you."

Jack and Ryan walked down the long corridor that led to the security room. Pressing the buzzer next to the door, they waited for Cumming. They didn't have to wait long.

Jack automatically reached out to shake the man's hand. "Mr. Cumming. Thank you for agreeing to see us."

Bryce waved aside the words. "It's not a problem. Please, have a seat," he said, gesturing to a couple of chairs.

Jack couldn't help but glance at a monitor that was running film footage from the museum's security cameras. He motioned to the video. "What are you doing?"

"Looking through the security tapes from the night Josh died. I was hoping that something would catch my attention. Something that may give insight to exactly what occurred."

"Did you notice anything?" Ryan asked.

Bryce ran a weary hand through his hair. "No. Everything looks normal. I confirmed that all the people here that night were scheduled to work. I checked the log books verifying the time they entered the museum, and what time they left. There are no red herrings."

"We understand that you paid a visit to Ken Light at the Americana Museum," Jack said.

"I did," Bryce admitted without reservation.

"Why?" Ryan asked.

"Because Josh used to work there, and he left under less than ideal circumstances. I wanted to investigate a little further to see what I could find out. To see if there might be a possible connection between what happened there and Josh's death."

"And did you find one?" Jack asked.

Bryce sat back in his chair. "Did I find one? I'm not sure exactly."

Jack's eyes narrowed slightly. "What do you mean?"

"I didn't realize that the woman convicted of the theft was a distant relative of Josh's," Bryce said.

Jack was a little surprised by the forthright response, but he was careful to keep his expression neutral. "Was she a relative of yours?" he asked bluntly.

"No."

"You sound very sure of that," Ryan replied.

"I'm positive."

"I take it you did the research to confirm the fact?" Jack questioned.

Bryce nodded. "I did. Gail Barret was a distant cousin of Josh's from his father's side. Not our mother's."

"It seemed a little strange that the woman tried to frame Josh, considering their relationship," Jack said, wondering what motivated her.

"Yeah, it does. And I've been sitting here all morning trying to come up with a reason. But I keep running into brick walls."

"How much research were you able to do?" Jack asked, knowing without being told that the man called in all favors to get an answer.

"Not much, I'm afraid. I was able to track down the phone numbers of some of my mother's relatives. I wanted to see if they might be able to fill in some blanks. But unfortunately, I was only able to leave messages. I haven't spoken to anybody yet."

"Please notify us if you find out anything," Ryan said.

"You two will be the first people I call. I want to find out what happened to Josh. You have my full cooperation in whatever you need to make that happen."

Jack nodded, accepting the sincerity. "I know this has been hard on you."

"It has been. Even though I didn't know Josh growing up, I did get to know him a little bit after I discovered our relationship. I never wanted to see anything happen to him. I owe it to Josh to help find his murderer. I owe it to my mother."

Chapter Seventeen

Later that evening, Jack was at home pouring over the information pertaining to the case relating to Josh Brody. Ashley wasn't home yet, she had left a message that she was delayed. She had met Amy Redding late that afternoon, and was stopping by the newspaper to pick up some information that Amy agreed to share.

Jack was looking at the photos that Ken Light had given them that day, when he heard the key in the door. Looking up, he caught sight of Ashley.

"Hi," he said, his eyes noticing the excitement shining in her eyes.

"Hi."

Jack placed the folder he was looking at on the sofa and rose to meet Ashley halfway across the room. "How was your day?" he asked, automatically reaching for the tote bag on her shoulder.

"Eventful. And yours?"

"The same. I take it your meeting with Amy went well?"

"Very. She told me about a theft that took place at the Americana Museum."

"Oh?"

"Did you know that Josh was related to the woman who actually committed the crime?"

"Yeah, I found that out today. Gail Barret, wasn't it?"

"Yes. How did you know?"

"Ryan and I stopped by the Americana Museum this morning. We met with Ken Light, the director of security. He told us."

Ashley kicked off her high-heeled shoes. "That's fascinating, isn't it?"

Jack shrugged, a smile playing about his lips at her obvious excitement about the information. One thing was certain. Ashley had in no way lost her enthusiasm for reporting. She still seemed to get a thrill out of uncovering stories. "Fascinating is a strong word. Interesting, maybe."

She laughed at his response, and walked over to the portable bar to get a bottle of water. Unscrewing the top, she took a long drink before walking to the sofa to sit down. "You can call it what you want, but it does prove that Josh was somehow related to the crime that took place there."

Jack frowned at her words, and took a seat across from her. "How do you figure that?"

"Josh was related to Gail."

"So? They were distant cousins from my understand-ing."

"Only from a bloodline point of view."

"What do you mean?"

"I mean that though they were fourth cousins, they were very close when they were growing up. Gail's family lived down the block from Josh's."

Jack frowned at the words and leaned forward in his chair. "Are you sure about that?"

"Amy's positive. She pulled all the files that the newspaper had on the incident. It's all there, in black and white."

"What do you mean?"

"Old family photographs," she replied, reaching for her tote bag and removing a file. She held it out to Jack. "Here. Take a look."

Inside the manila folder Jack discovered several pho-tos of people, along with handwritten notes from the reporter that covered the story. "Can Amy get into trou-ble for giving you this?"

"She could, if anybody found out about it. But she trusts me to make sure that we don't reveal the source."

Jack nodded slightly, his full attention on the informa-tion in his hand. "It says here that Gail Barret came from a large family, with several step-brothers and sisters."

"Yes. Her mother remarried at least three times."

"It doesn't list all of the children's names."

"No, unfortunately, a lot of the kids were much older than Gail. Either they were already out on their own when this research was done, or they were living with their biological fathers."

"And how did you come to the conclusion that Josh was somehow related to the theft that took place at the Americana Museum?"

"If Gail was as close to Josh as those notes indicate, it would stand to reason that Josh was aware that Gail was up to something. Maybe they argued about what she was doing, which might explain why she tried to implicate him in the crime."

"Out of spite?" Jack asked.

"Yes."

"I admit that it's a plausible possibility, but all of this wouldn't explain why there was so much animosity between Josh and Andrew Carstair."

"Andrew was the assistant curator at the museum at the time of the theft."

"So?"

"So, his ambition was to be appointed curator. The theft at the museum pretty much guaranteed that wasn't going to happen."

"Was there a possibility that it would?"

Ashley shifted slightly on the sofa, moving to a more comfortable position. "Yes. The curator of the museum was out on family leave. There was an illness in his family that might have forced him to move to Washington state. Andrew would have been in line for the promotion."

"Until this happened."

"That's right."

"Was Andrew aware of the relationship Josh and Gail shared?"

"He was. It came out during the investigation. Gail went full force in trying to pin the theft on Josh."

"Which would have left a bitter taste in Andrew's mouth."

Ashley lifted one shoulder in a shrug. "I think it would be a safe bet that there would have been some resentment on his end. I mean think about it. The World Museum is a great steppingstone in Andrew's life, but the Americana Museum would have been a bigger feather in his cap. It's a major museum in Manhattan. If he had been curator there, he would have been able to write his own ticket with regard to his career. I think it would be a natural reaction for him to have some resentment toward Josh. To blame him for what happened."

"The man would have had the motive to kill Brody," Jack acknowledged.

"And opportunity."

"Yes. But only if he would have been able to somehow bypass security. The log book isn't showing that he was in the museum around the time of Brody's death."

"I would think that if anybody would be able to gain access to the museum undetected, it would have been Andrew."

"Knowing that and proving that are two different things," Jack said.

Ashley noticed Jack's preoccupation. "There are still a lot of unanswered questions."

"More than I'd like."

"I know. I thought I would try and track down further information tomorrow."

"How?"

"I'll make some calls and collect on a few favors. Maybe something else will surface that will help with the investigation."

"I don't want you getting too involved in this, Ash. There's someone out there who took great pains to cover their steps the night Brody was killed. They can't find out that you're searching for answers."

Ashley rolled her eyes at his words. "I know."

"I'm serious."

"I know you are, Jack. And I'll be careful."

"No chances."

"None," she agreed softly.

He nodded and turned his attention back to the file in his hand. "I'm having a full background report done on Gail Barret also. With any luck, I'll have some answers tomorrow."

Ashley was silent for a moment before asking, "How's Ryan handling all this?"

Jack shrugged. "All right."

"Good. I was a little worried about him."

"Why? Because of Jane?"

"Yes. His attention has to be a little distracted."

"Ryan's a professional. He's able to put personal feelings aside during an investigation."

"I still feel bad for him."

"I wouldn't worry too much about him. Ryan can handle anything that comes his way."

Chapter Eighteen

The following morning, Jack met Ryan for breakfast at a diner near the police station. The place was packed. Taking a seat at a booth in the back, they watched as the waitresses scrambled around the room attempting to cater to everybody's demands.

"It's busy here today," Jack remarked as a waitress accidentally bumped into their table.

Ryan grunted. "Yeah, but the food is good. A little noise is a small price to pay for an edible meal."

Jack smiled at Ryan's response and picked up a menu. "What are you having?"

"Pancakes," Ryan replied without opening his own menu.

Jack closed his menu and placed it back into its holder. "Sounds good," he said as a waitress came by to fill their coffee cups and take their orders. As soon as she left, he asked, "How's Jane doing?"

Ryan shrugged. "All right. She's much better than she was."

"Did you see her last night?"

"Yeah, we had dinner," Ryan said before admitting, "I brought up the subject of our going to the Americana Museum."

"Oh?" Jack asked, curious about why Ryan had done that. He was usually more circumspect in his actions. Ryan was fully aware that Jane had still not been eliminated as a possible suspect in Brody's murder.

Ryan's eyes met Jack's as if reading his thoughts. "I wanted to see if she could add any more insight to what we found out."

Jack nodded and took a sip of his coffee. "And?"

"And, she said Andrew had mentioned about a week ago that Josh was getting a little too cocky for his own good."

Jack's eyes narrowed. "Those were her words?"

"She's stating they were Andrew's."

"It's a strange thing to say."

"I agree. Apparently, she thought so too, because she asked the man to expand on the comment."

"And what did he say?"

"According to Jane, Andrew thought Josh was trying to take over control of the Egyptian exhibition. He was concerned that Josh was overstepping bounds. That he was trying to take credit for the design behind the exhibition."

"And did Jane think he was?" Jack asked just as the waitress delivered their breakfast.

Ryan waited until the waitress left. "She claims no."

Jack zeroed in on the word 'claims.' "You don't believe her?" he asked, catching the note of uncertainty in Ryan's voice, in his choice of words.

Ryan expelled a harsh breath and reached for the syrup. "No."

"Why not?"

"Because she's too smart not to realize what the man was doing. I really believe that Josh was trying to take over the exhibition."

"What would he have to gain by it?"

"Recognition. You saw the press coverage the night of the opening. If this exhibition had opened without a hitch, Josh would have fully regained the good use of his name."

"Which was damaged in the scandal at the Americana Museum," Jack finished.

"Exactly."

"Thinking that the man had ulterior motives is a harsh stance to take."

"But accurate I'm afraid."

"Did Jane ever mention any of this previously?"

"You mean prior to the murder?" Ryan asked, trying to clarify the question.

"Yes."

Ryan shook his head. "She didn't give a clue."

"Maybe it didn't bother her?"

Ryan took a sip of his coffee. "It had to."

"Why? Because it bothers you?"

"No. Because it would be an honest reaction."

"People react differently to circumstances. Maybe Jane was so sure of her position at the museum that she didn't feel threatened by the guy."

"Maybe."

Jack watched Ryan closely. "You look like you're having a hard time buying that."

"I am. And that bothers me."

"Do you think Jane is hiding something from you?"

Ryan took a moment to think about Jack's question. "Not intentionally."

"Unintentionally?"

"I think that's a strong possibility. I mean think about it. If Jane wasn't threatened by Josh, she had to have a reason for it. And the only one that makes sense is that she was so sure of her position at the museum that she knew that Josh could never be a threat to her. A nuisance maybe, but not a threat. She had to know that her job was secure. That nothing could ever happen that would take away from her getting credit for the exhibition's design."

"Confidence in her own ability would have ensured that."

Ryan nodded, finding truth in Jack's words. "And nobody can claim Jane lacked talent."

"No, they can't." Jack was trying to be careful with what he said until all the facts of the case presented themselves.

Ryan was quiet for a moment before admitting, "Maybe I'm reading too much into this." He hated the direction that his thoughts had gone. He hated that he was starting to doubt Jane. The fact that he was beginning to think that she was somehow involved in Josh's death tore at his gut. But he also knew that he wouldn't be able to rest until all the avenues in the investigation had been covered.

"Things will eventually sort themselves out. Don't knock yourself out before we have the facts."

"That's easier said than done," Ryan replied, letting some of his frustration show.

"It's hard investigating a case when you have a personal stake in it," Jack said, letting Ryan know that he was aware of where he was coming from. Of where his mindset was. "Want a word of advice?"

"Sure."

"Don't let anybody see that this is bothering you. They'll have you twisting every which way in the wind if you let them catch even a glimpse of it."

"I'm already under the gun from Ed about Jane's connection in this."

"He's just doing his job. He knows there's not going to be any conflict from you."

"He should."

"He does," Jack said before catching sight of the crowd by the door. "It looks like there's a group of people waiting to be seated. Maybe we should finish up here and head out so that someone else can have our table."

Ryan glanced back to the door. "Sound like a good idea," he said, picking up his fork and beginning to eat his meal.

Chapter Nineteen

Later that morning, Jack and Ryan were scrutinizing the evidence tagged in the case.

"Did you find anything yet that we may have missed in the initial search?" Ryan asked as he rifled through articles taken from Brody's residence.

"Not much. You?"

"No. Nothing that's going to solve this case."

"This is just a long shot anyway."

"True," Ryan said, placing some of the evidence in a different box for sorting purposes. "What time are we supposed to get the background report on Gail Barret?"

Jack glanced at his watch. "They promised that it would be done around eleven."

"It's almost that time now."

"Well, if they didn't run into any problems in pulling the information, it should be here soon."

Ryan nodded. "What's Ashley doing today?"

Jack grimaced. "Research."

Ryan smirked at Jack's expression. "On this case?"

"What else?"

"She still has her desire to dig for dirt, huh?"

"Unfortunately, I think it's an ingrained part of who she is."

"There are worse things."

"There are also safer things."

"I'm sure she'll be careful."

Jack grunted just as the phone rang. He reached for the receiver. "Reeves."

"Jack?" Ashley asked, her voice loud and clear.

"Hi, babe. What's up?"

"I wanted to know if you and Ryan could meet me at the house."

"Now?"

There was the sound of shuffling in the background before she responded. "Yes. Can you come?"

Jack glanced at his watch once more. The report on Gail Barret was scheduled to arrive at any moment, and he really wanted to look at it as soon as possible. "Is this something that can wait until I get home?"

"No. I think it's important. It pertains to Josh Brody's murder."

"You found out something?"

"Yeah, but I can't tell you about it on the phone. It's something that you need to see."

"Can you bring it to the station?"

"I would, but I'm also waiting for a fax that I think

might help you with the case. I'm hoping it will be here by the time you arrive."

"All right," Jack said, curious about what she had been able to find out. He glanced at his watch. "We'll see you in half an hour."

"Okay. See you then," Ashley said, disconnecting the call.

Ryan glanced at Jack as soon as he placed the receiver back in the cradle. "What's up?"

"That was Ashley. She wants us to come to the house."

"Is everything all right?" Ryan asked with concern.

"Yeah. She said she had some information about Brody."

Ryan frowned. "Did she say what?"

"No. She said she couldn't tell me on the phone. Are you up to a trip to the house?"

Ryan placed all the items he was sorting through back in the boxes. "I'm right behind you."

Thirty minutes later, Jack opened the front door to his house. "Ash?" he called out. He heard her footsteps on the stairwell upstairs, and he glanced up to catch her looking down at them.

"I'm coming," she promised, quickly descending the stairs. She smiled at Ryan the moment she saw him hovering in the background. "Hi, Ryan," she greeted warmly.

"Hi, Ashley."

"It's good to see you."

Ryan smiled. "Yeah, you too."

She reached for Jack's hand and led him into the kitchen. "Come see what I found."

Jack let her lead him into the kitchen and over to the table. He frowned as he noticed newspaper clippings covering the top. They were all from an out-of-town paper. "What's this?"

"Josh's hometown paper," she responded.

"What?" Ryan asked, stepping up beside Jack to get his own look at the articles. There were ones dated several years back, as well as current ones reporting Josh's death.

"One of my contacts had these. He was covering Josh's murder and he took a trip back to Josh's hometown upstate. He was able to meet with the reporter covering the story, and she was gracious enough to give him this for his piece."

Jack absently nodded, and reached for one of the articles. "This is on Gail Barret," he said, looking at the grainy photograph displayed.

"Yes. When her story first broke, the local paper did an expose on her. That's a picture of her family at a local town picnic about ten years ago," Ashley said.

Ryan glanced at the photo. "Can I see that?"

"Sure," Jack said, handing over the photograph and picking up another article to look at.

"One of these people looks familiar," Ryan said as he studied the picture.

Jack frowned. "Familiar?"

"Yeah. The guy in the top row, two people over from the left."

Jack once again reached for the photo. "Let me see."

Ashley rested her hand on Jack's suit jacket as she also looked at the photograph. "Ryan's right. I've seen that person before."

"Where?" Jack asked.

"I'm not sure," she replied. "You have to remember that the photograph is old. Ten years old. People change. Any little change in the person's weight would make a big difference in how a person would photograph. And then there's the fact that the guy is bald. We're not sure whether that's due to nature or preference."

"We could take it down to the station and see if they can scan the photograph into the computer. Maybe if we make some changes to the person's looks, we'll be able to determine who the man is," Jack suggested.

"Sounds like a plan to me," Ryan said.

"It shouldn't take that long to do. The problem that's going to arise is whether or not they're going to be able to get a clear enough scan from the paper. The quality isn't great."

"Anything's worth a shot," Ryan replied.

"I agree with Ryan," Ashley said.

Jack nodded. "What else did you manage to find?" he asked, sorting through the rest of the documents.

Ashley reached for an article on Josh's death. "This is the fax I was waiting on. It's an article that's due to run in tomorrow's edition of the paper. It has a reference to the tie between Gail Barret and Josh. The connection of family, as well as the facts of the theft at the Americana Museum."

Ryan read it. After he was done, he handed it to Jack. "Hometown news. There's nothing like it," Ryan said disparagingly.

"It's public interest," Ashley responded.

"But it shouldn't be. By airing dirty laundry in the press like this, you make it virtually impossible for any other family members living in the town to go about their daily business without scrutiny."

"The public has a right to know what's going on."

"The press has the responsibility to report news. Not take the story off on a tangent that only serves as sensationalism."

Ashley opened her mouth to retort, and quickly closed it. Understanding dawned. "Jane is getting hounded by reporters?" she asked sympathetically, realizing that Ryan was more bothered by this case than he let on. That contrary to what people thought, he was having a hard time separating his work from his concern for Jane's well-being.

Ryan grimaced. "Nonstop."

"I'm sorry."

"Why? It's not your fault."

"No, but I do sympathize with her."

"So do I. She's not used to negative attention. Right now, they're asking her all kinds of questions about Josh and his role at the museum. Some airhead actually had the nerve to ask her if she was threatened by Josh's talent."

Ashley cringed. "There are a lot of people who don't think before they speak."

"Ain't that the truth."

"Things will get better. Just tell Jane to hang in there. Once the heat from the story dies down, things will begin to go back to normal."

Ryan lifted a shoulder expressively. "I hope so."

"I know," Ashley said, reaching for a clasp envelope on the table. She began to put the pictures and articles into it. "Are you guys hungry?" she asked, deciding that it would be a good idea to change the subject.

Jack turned to Ryan. "Ry?"

Ryan groaned. "I'm still full from breakfast."

Ashley smiled sympathetically and turned to Jack. "Do you want something to eat?"

"No, thanks."

"Coffee?"

Jack smiled and took the envelope from her hand. "Not right now. We need to get back to the station. I'm waiting for a report to come in. But thanks for getting this information. It's going to be a bigger help than you realize."

"No problem."

Jack brushed a stray piece of hair away from her cheek. "We'll go out to dinner tonight. You can think of where you'd like to eat."

"I don't have to think about it."

"Palermo's?"

"It's my favorite."

"If that's where you want to go, you'd better call and make reservations. You know tonight's one of their busiest nights."

"I will. Call me when you're on your way home tonight. I'll try to be ready by the time you arrive."

"Okay," he said, dropping a light kiss on her cheek before heading toward the door with Ryan. "See you later."

Chapter Twenty

The moment Jack and Ryan arrived back at the police precinct, Ed called them into his office.

"What's up?" Jack asked as he took a seat.

Ed tapped the file on his desktop. "Gail Barret's preliminary background report arrived."

Ryan reached for it. "What does it say?"

"Read it for yourself," Ed instructed, settling back in his chair as Ryan began scanning the pages.

"It doesn't look like there's a lot here."

"Keep reading. There's some pertinent information in there. They had some trouble getting everything together for the time promised, but they sent over what they could. Apparently, there's a large extended family that will take a little longer to research."

"How large of a family?" Jack asked.

"Eight in all."

"Eight?" Jack asked, automatically reaching for the envelope he had picked up from Ashley. He pulled out the article with the family photograph, and looked at it briefly before handing it to Ed. "This might be a photo of them all."

Ed looked at it, noting that it was from several years back and from an out-of-town newspaper. "Where did you happen to get this?"

"Ashley."

Ed's eyebrows rose slightly. "Can I ask where she got it from?"

"One of her contacts."

"No need to say more. The quality of the picture isn't that great."

"No, it's not. We were hoping that one of our specialists might be able to do something with it."

Ed nodded and continued to look at the photograph. "We may be able to convert it to a digital format and get a clearer enhancement of the picture."

"That's what we were hoping for."

"After we're through here, head over to see Marco. We'll see what he can do," Ed said.

"Sure," Jack agreed, before looking over at Ryan and noticing his preoccupation as he continued to read through the file. "What has you so quiet?"

Ryan didn't answer Jack's comment directly, instead he looked over at Ed. "Did you read this?"

Ed nodded.

Ryan maintained eye contact with Ed for a brief moment before handing the report to Jack. "Here. Take a look."

Jack frowned and did as he requested. "Gail Barret's father worked for the poison control agency," he said.

"That's right," Ed acknowledged.

Jack looked over at Ed. "Do we know where he is? Maybe he had something to do with this."

"He had a stroke about a month ago. He's still recovering."

"What about his other kids? They might have known where to obtain the cyanide that was used to kill Brody. We might be dealing with one of Gail Barret's siblings."

"That's a possibility. And there's something else. I spoke to the district attorney's office. More important, to the prosecutor assigned to Barret's case. It looks like Josh Brody was ready to turn state's evidence against the woman."

"Which would solidify a motive by her family," Ryan said.

Ed nodded and motioned to the file. "Unfortunately, that report is only listing the basics right now. Due to the fact that Barret's mother remarried so much, we're having a little trouble tracking down all of the siblings. They're hoping to have the information available by tonight."

"I never thought that one of Gail's relatives might be involved in Josh's murder. Especially considering that they were also related to Josh," Ryan said.

"They were only related distantly," Jack reminded him.

Ryan motioned to the photograph that Ed held. "One of the people in that photograph looks familiar."

Ed frowned. "Which one?"

"The man in the top row, two people over from the left."

"Do you know where you saw him?"

"No, I can't pinpoint that. At least not yet. I just know there's something about him that I recognize."

"Ashley thought the same thing," Jack said.

Ed looked at Jack. "She couldn't place him either?"

"No. Like Ryan, she recognizes something about the man's features, but she can't pinpoint what it is."

Ed glanced back down at the photograph. "Maybe with some computer enhancing we'll be able to confirm the identity."

"Let's hope so. Because if Ryan and Ashley both found something familiar about the man, there's a good possibility that the guy was present at the museum the night we found Brody's body," Jack replied.

"Which might mean he would have had something to do with Brody's death," Ryan said.

Ed's gaze encompassed both men. "You may have something there," he agreed, handing the photo back to Jack before he reached for the phone. "Maybe you guys should head over to see Marco now. I'll call him and tell him you're on the way over. The faster we start this process, the faster we'll have answers."

"Do you think Marco will have the time to play around with this right now?" Ryan asked.

"He'll make the time," Ed assured.

Jack stood to his feet. "We'll call you if we're able to determine anything."

"All right. And I'll call you if the rest of the reports come in."

Five minutes later, they entered the computer lab where Marco Santiago worked. The lab was quiet, most of the personnel were out to lunch, and Marco was working diligently at his desk when they walked up to him.

"Marco," Jack greeted.

Marco turned at the sound of his name, a smile crossing his features as he caught sight of them. "Hey. Long time no see."

"It has been awhile. How's the family?"

"Good. And Ashley? How's she feeling?"

"Pretty good."

"I'm glad."

"Ed call you?"

"Yes, he did," Marco responded, kicking his chair back from his desk and holding out a hand for the envelope that Jack held. "Is that the picture?"

Jack nodded and withdrew the article. "Yeah."

Marco studied the poor quality of the photo. "This is going to be hard to convert to a digital format, but we'll try."

"If anybody would be able to, it would be you," Ryan said.

Within minutes, Marco had a digital image of the photograph in the computer.

"It's still unclear."

"Patience," Marco said as he played around with the image until he cleared it up.

"Can you zero in on the man two people from the left, top row?" Ryan asked, squinting as he tried to identify where he had seen the man before.

"Sure. Any better?"

Ryan studied the photograph for a little longer before shaking his head. "I still can't place the guy."

Marco glanced down at the image. "This photograph is old."

"About ten years."

"Let me try something." Marco transferred an image of the man to a separate file, and computer-aged the image. "How's this?"

"Not much better."

"Let's try dropping some weight."

"Still not yet," Ryan said.

"How about if we add some hair?"

Jack watched as the image changed, and something about the photo caught his attention. "Change the color of the hair to dark brown streaked with gray," he ordered.

"Sure."

Jack's eyes narrowed. "That's Dane Trevor."

Chapter Twenty-One

Jack immediately reached for the phone on Marco's desk and dialed Ed's extension. "We have an identification," he said the moment Ed answered. "Dane Trevor. A security guard who works at the museum. He was there the night we found Brody's body."

"Do we have the background check on him?" Ed asked.

"We have what Bryce Cumming gave us, and our preliminary report. Nothing stood out. The guy's highly regarded in his circle. He's worked for some major firms."

"But nothing that connected him to Gail Barret?"

"No, at least not under that name. It's possible we're dealing with an alias though," Jack said.

"You call and arrange to bring the guy in for

questioning. I'm going to get on the line now and demand that they rush the full background check on him. Hopefully, I'll have something this afternoon."

Jack glanced at his watch. "Let me see what I can do," he said, before disconnecting.

"What's going on?" Ryan asked.

"Ed's going to rush a detailed report on the guy. There was nothing with the information we have, or the information Bryce gave us that made any connection between Dane Trevor and Brody. There has to be more here than meets the eye."

Ryan nodded and turned to Marco. "Do us a favor. Backup that file and print us a clear copy of all the versions of the photograph."

Marco performed the requested task and handed the photographs to Ryan.

"Thanks."

"Don't mention it."

Ryan looked at Jack. "Do you think Dane Trevor is working today?"

"There's one way to find out," Jack said, placing a call to Bryce Cumming at the museum. He was on the phone for little over a minute.

"What did Bryce say?" Ryan asked.

"Dane Trevor is off today."

"That means we have only one option open."

"Yeah. We'll need to arrange for a search warrant on the guy's residence. Let's head back to our area and get the ball rolling on that. With any luck, we'll have it within the hour."

"Let's go."

A couple of hours later, Jack and Ryan were parked outside Dane Trevor's house. The small colonial-style house stood on a little over an acre of property in a heavily wooded area on eastern Long Island.

Ryan shifted slightly in his seat to unbuckle his seat belt while he peered at the house. He noticed the peeling paint of the clapboard, the slightly crooked shutters that framed the windows. The yard was overgrown with weeds and shrubbery, and the grass was long overdue to be mowed. "It looks a little run down," he observed.

"Yeah, it does. Maybe the man has had other things on his mind lately other than taking care of his property."

"Like what? Murder?"

"You said it."

Ryan continued to glance around the property. "It doesn't look like Trevor is home."

"No, it doesn't. But since we have no idea of where he is, there's always the chance that he's on his way home."

"I guess we'll soon find out," Ryan said, noticing that the crime scene investigators had arrived. He watched as they exited the van and unloaded equipment, then he faced Jack. "It looks like it's showtime."

"That it does. Come on. Let's get going. The sooner we get started, the faster we'll finish."

It took only a few minutes to gain access to the house. Entering through the living room, they noticed the old, heavy furniture, the cracked plaster on the wall.

"Housekeeping doesn't seem to be this guy's strong suit," Ryan said, while pulling on a pair of latex gloves.

"No, but his domestic accomplishments aren't what we're after," Jack reminded him as he began walking through the room and opening drawers, searching through the contents.

"You look here, I'll go upstairs. Yell if you find anything."

"You got it," Jack said, not looking up from his task.

An hour later, Jack finished searching the living room. The crime scene technicians were spread out on the property, looking for anything that would tie Trevor to Brody's murder. So far, the search had turned up nothing.

Ryan met Jack as he finished going through the man's open mail on a desk. "Find anything?" Ryan asked.

"Not yet," Jack replied, sorting through the numerous bills.

"I just checked with the guys taking apart the bedroom. They came up empty-handed."

"No photographs hanging around?"

"Not one."

"It would have been nice to find a photograph to match the one Marco had been able to produce."

"That would have made our life a lot easier," Ryan acknowledged.

Jack stepped back from the desk. "Did you search the attic?"

"Yeah. It's not used. Other than some old insulation, there's nothing there."

"I'm trying to think. When did our background report state that Dane Trevor bought this house?"

"A little over a year ago."

"And he has nothing stored in the attic?"

"No, it's clean. I checked it myself."

"And the basement?" Jack asked.

"The house has a cellar, and the entryway is outside. It's locked tighter than a drum. One of the technicians just went to retrieve the bolt cutters. They should be just getting access about now."

"Then let's go join them."

Once outside, they immediately saw three officers standing outside the cellar doors, cutting through a heavy gauge chain.

"It looks like the guy might have something valuable down there," Jack murmured.

"Maybe he's just the cautious type."

"Maybe."

Ryan stepped forward the moment the chain had been cut away from the door. "We'll soon find out."

The cellar was dark and damp as Jack and Ryan made their way down the rickety steps, and the sound of mice scurrying to hide from the light was distinct in the otherwise quiet enclosure.

Jack flicked on a flashlight. Shining the bright beam of light throughout the cellar, he searched for a light fixture. "It would help if we had more light on the area."

Ryan moved forward with his own flashlight. "I think I see a fixture," he said, reaching out to pull the chain that generated the electricity.

The small-wattage bulb in the old tin fixture cast just enough light so they could see five feet in front of them.

"That wasn't much help," Jack muttered.

"No, but between that light and our flashlights, we should be able to at least get a feel for what's down here."

"You mean other than mice," Jack said as he began investigating the far wall. Shining his beam against the surface, he skimmed the light quickly past an area before pausing. "Ryan?"

"Yeah?"

"Go get the bolt cutters from the guy upstairs. There's a door here that has a padlock."

Ryan was back in a minute. "Do you want to do the honors or should I?"

"If you're up to it, be my guest."

Ryan clamped the padlock in between the cutters and applied the force necessary to break the lock. He cast it aside and opened the door. "I think I found a light switch," he said. His eyes widened at the small laboratory set up in the basement.

"Well, well," Jack murmured as he stepped into the room, his eyes taking in all of the paraphernalia on the tables.

Ryan began to walk around the room, noticing the scales, test tubes, and beakers that lined the shelves. "It looks like Dane Trevor had a hobby."

"You can say that again," Jack said as he walked up to a table that had several notebooks piled up.

Ryan watched as Jack opened the cover on one book. "What's in there?"

Jack glanced through the book. "Formulas. It looks like our friend dabbled in chemistry."

"Which might just tie him into Josh's murder."

"It might. At the very least, the man has a lot of explaining to do."

"Too bad we don't know where's he's at. We could go and pick him up for questioning."

"Maybe Bryce Cumming has a way of reaching the guy. I'm going to go upstairs and make the call. I don't think I'll pick up a signal on my cell phone down here."

"All right. And while you're doing that, we'll start packing up this stuff," Ryan replied.

"Okay," Jack said, leaving to make the call. It was ten minutes before he returned.

Ryan glanced in Jack's direction. "Well? Did you have any luck?"

"There was no need to make the call."

"Why not?"

"Dane Trevor just pulled in the driveway. He's fit to be tied."

Chapter Twenty-Two

A couple of hours later, Jack and Ryan were sitting across the table from Dane in one of the interrogation rooms.

"Does the name Gail Barret mean anything to you?" Jack asked, watching Dane carefully as the man met his gaze head on. After his initial shock at finding out that the police had searched his residence, a calmness had settled over him. It was a strong indication that he wasn't going to willingly confess to Brody's murder.

"Just what I read in the newspapers," Dane replied. He looked at the packet of cigarettes that rested on the table. "May I?"

"Help yourself," Jack said, having the foresight of having the cigarettes on hand after Bryce Cumming mentioned on the phone that Dane smoked.

Dane cupped his hand around the lighter as he lit the

cigarette. "What do I have to do with Gail Barret?" he asked, watching Jack and Ryan through a cloud of smoke.

"We were hoping you would tell us," Ryan replied.

Dane studied both men silently for a moment. "I can't tell you what I don't know."

Jack nodded and picked up a folder. "Maybe this will help jog your memory," he said, pulling out the newspaper article that had the picture of Barret's family. The one that Marco had been able to enhance to reveal Dane.

Dane took a drag off his cigarette and narrowed his eyes to study the picture. "This is supposed to mean something to me?"

"It doesn't?" Ryan questioned.

"No, I can't say that it does."

"What about the second person from the left in the top row? Does he look familiar?"

"I can't say that I know him."

"Are you sure?" Jack asked, pushing the photograph closer to Dane. "Take a better look."

Dane studied the photograph for a long moment before pushing it back to Jack. "Sorry. The image is fuzzy. I can't make out the guy's features."

"Fair enough," Jack said, reaching for another picture. "Actually, we thought that might be the case, so we took the liberty of having one of our experts enhance the photo in the lab. They were lucky enough to get a clear image. Maybe this one will ring a bell."

Dane watched as Jack slid another photo across the

table. "It is clearer, but unfortunately I still can't identify the man."

"Still?" Ryan asked doubtfully.

"Sorry."

"That's okay. We have one more photograph that
we're hoping will help with your memory," Jack said,
reaching for the age-enhanced photo that pinpointed
Dane as the individual in question. "How about this
one?"

Dane stilled as the image of himself rested on the
table before him. "Is this some sort of joke?"

"We're not laughing," Jack assured him, feeling a
certain amount of satisfaction at being able to shake the
man's composure.

Dane pushed the photograph roughly back to Jack.
"Everybody knows that you can do whatever you want
with a computer. There are all types of photographic
programs available that will allow you to alter pictures.
This picture means nothing."

"Are you sure?" Ryan asked.

"Are you?" Dane shot back. "My attorney's going to
have a field day with this. As a matter of fact, I want
him in here right now. If you guys are accusing me of
something, I have a right for him to be here."

Jack pushed a phone across the desk. "Be my guest.
Call him."

"I'd like some privacy."

"Sure. We'll go and get a cup of coffee," Ryan said.
"Would you like something?"

"No."

"We'll wait until your attorney gets here before we continue," Jack said, and left.

"What do you think?" Ryan asked the moment the door closed behind them.

Jack shrugged and rubbed the back of his neck. "I think the photograph threw him a lot more than he's willing to let on right now."

"I agree. It'll be interesting to see how long he's going to be able to deny knowing Gail Barret."

Jack glanced at his watch. "Look, while we're waiting for his attorney to show up, I'm going to go and check with Ed. I want to see if any of the reports we were waiting for came in."

"Okay. I'll hold things down here."

Jack walked into Ed's office without knocking. "Hey."

"Hi," Ed replied, leaning back in his chair. "How's it going with Trevor? Did he say anything yet?"

"No. He requested his attorney."

"Sounds like he's nervous."

"Or just smart."

"He's not talking at all?"

"No."

"Well, nobody said this was going to be easy."

"No, they didn't," Jack admitted, looking at the folders spread out on Ed's desk. "What are you doing?"

"Just reviewing what we have on the guy so far. I pulled the information that the museum had on him. His record is spotless."

"Yeah, I know. But there has to be some sort of connection between the man and Brody's murder. It's the only thing that makes sense. Especially if you take into consideration that makeshift lab we found at his house, and his appearance in the family photograph with Gail Barret."

"Yeah, I know. I tried calling the newspaper upstate to see if I could get a phone number for the photographer that took the original picture that connected Trevor to this mess. I thought it might be worth a shot to see if we could talk to him."

"Any luck?"

"No, the guy died five years back. Heart attack."

Jack opened his mouth to speak just as the fax machine by Ed's desk rang.

Ed swiveled around in his chair and watched the page begin to print. "It's the report on Trevor."

"How many pages?"

"The cover page says seven."

"Sounds like they found something out."

"Yeah. But now we have to see if it's worth anything."

As soon as the machine signaled that it was through, Ed picked up the report and put the pages in order. He was silent for several minutes while he read.

"Well?" Jack asked.

"There's definitely a connection between Gail Barret and Dane Trevor, but it's not the connection we thought."

Jack reached for the pages. "He's not her brother?"

"No. He's her biological father."

Chapter Twenty-Three

"This I didn't expect," Jack said, beginning to read the report for himself.

"No. I thought for sure he was going to be a sibling."

"It says here that he was never married to her mother."

"Which might explain why this didn't show up right away. The man's not listed on her birth certificate. From all indications, this was something they were trying to keep a secret. Probably due to the fact that they were never married. Small towns tend to have strict ideals about acceptable behavior."

"It makes you wonder how Gail's mother explained the pregnancy."

"She didn't have to. If you read the third page of the report, it states that she married her high school sweetheart, Kevin Barret, before anyone could put two and two together. Apparently the two of them had dated off and on throughout their high school years, so nobody questioned the suddenness of the marriage. People probably just put it down to the impulsiveness of youth."

Jack was silent while he read. "How were we able to trace this?" he asked, looking through the pages for the information.

"The fourth page lists the source. Apparently Gail Barret mentioned it to prison officials when she had an argument with Kevin Barret, the man who's listed as her father on her birth certificate. She didn't want him visiting her anymore, and she told the authorities over there that Dane Trevor was her biological father. Her mother must have told her the truth somewhere along the way."

Jack continued to read. "There's a copy of his college transcript. The man took several courses in chemistry and biopharmaceuticals."

"I saw that. He would definitely know a thing or two about cyanide and how it affects the body."

"And he apparently has enough contacts where he could have obtained the cyanide on the outside."

"That's right. This all points to one person as Josh Brody's killer."

Jack nodded. "He had the motive. His daughter was turned into the authorities by Josh. And he also had the opportunity. He was working at the museum the night of the murder."

"He also had full security clearance. That alone

bought him full access to the museum, as well as the time to carry out the crime. He knew exactly when to make his move."

Jack finished glancing through the report and laid it on Ed's desk. "We'll need a confession. This is all circumstantial evidence."

"Do you think you can get one?"

"I'm going to try."

Two hours later, Jack and Ryan were once again sitting across the table from Trevor and his attorney, Mitch Stevens, who had only arrived fifteen minutes ago. The preliminary report had come in on the makeshift lab in the man's basement, and it confirmed that cyanide was present.

Jack leaned forward in his chair, going over the events that Trevor stated occurred on the night of Brody's murder. He had yet to drop the bombshell about their find. He wanted to see if the man would open up on his own without him saying it. He began to review what Trevor had said. "Let me get this straight. You're saying that you arrived for your shift at around eleven P.M. on the night that Josh was murdered."

Dane nodded. "That's correct."

"How many people were working in the museum that night?" Jack asked, watching every nuance of the man's movements, every shift of his eyes.

"By the time I got there?" Dane asked.

"Yes."

"About ten. People were already going home. The

copy of the log book that Bryce gave you should verify that."

Jack didn't deny or confirm the man's statement. "And did you see Josh at all during this time?"

"No."

"Would your path have normally crossed with his?" Ryan questioned.

Dane shrugged. "Not necessarily. There were three of us working that night for security. I never had a reason to go to the wing that Josh was working in."

"Did you have a reason to go to the cafeteria?" Jack asked.

Dane looked startled by the question. "Of course."

"What time did you visit the room?"

"About midnight. Why?"

"Because we have reason to believe that Josh visited it around the same time," Jack replied.

"Well, he wasn't there when I arrived."

"You didn't pass him in the halls?" Ryan asked.

"No."

"Did you have any problems with Josh? Did you hold any resentment against the man?" Jack asked.

"Why would I?"

"Maybe because he was ready to turn state's evidence against Gail Barret. Your daughter," Jack replied, watching Dane carefully as he made the statement, noticing the sudden paling of his complexion.

At the comment, Mitch Stevens glanced sharply at Dane, but Dane ignored the look. "You don't know what you're talking about."

"Your daughter is the one who made the statement."

"Gail Barret told you that she was my daughter?"

"Are you denying it?"

When Dane didn't respond, Jack pushed. "Well?"

Dane took his time in replying, as if thinking about the right words to say. "I admit that I dated Gail's mother. But that was a long time ago. If Gail is claiming a relationship with me, she's conning you."

"There's a way to disprove her statement. We can do a simple DNA test," Jack said.

Dane was silent for a long moment before saying, "Maybe that's a good idea. If Gail Barret is related to me, I have a right to know."

Jack's eyes narrowed slightly at Dane's words. The man was still playing the part of total innocence. "You're saying you didn't know this?"

"No."

"And you're still denying that it's you who's in the family photograph of Gail Barret's family?" Ryan asked.

"Yes."

"Then there's just one more thing that we need clarification on," Jack said.

"What's that?"

"Explain why you have a laboratory set up in your basement, and why the poison that killed Josh Brody was present."

Dane stiffened. Mitch Stevens glanced at Dane and motioned for him to remain quiet. "Don't say anything further."

Jack saw the blind panic in Dane's eyes, he sensed the entrapment that the man felt. "Talk to me, Dane. We know you killed Brody. We know it was because you felt your daughter was betrayed. Let us help you. If you cooperate with us, it might go easier on you."

Dane reached for another cigarette with a hand that trembled slightly. "I had nothing to do with Josh's death."

"Maybe you don't realize exactly what's at stake here," Jack shot back. "We're talking murder one. We're talking the possibility of the death penalty. We have the evidence against you. There's no way you're not going down for Brody's murder. The only question that remains is how hard are you willing to fall?"

Tension filled the room and Mitch turned to Dane, hoping to get a moment alone with his client. "Dane, we need to talk."

Dane didn't hear Mitch, his full concentration was on Jack. "You're grasping at straws," he said, his jaw clenching on the words.

Jack noticed that Dane totally ignored Mitch. It was as if he was no longer aware of the man's presence in the room. He saw the way that Dane was focused on him, and he sensed that there was something in his words that hit a nerve. The panic that had been in his eyes only moments earlier was being overshadowed with anger, and his body language and tone of voice hinted at an aggression simmering below the surface. Jack knew at that moment that he had the advantage, that the right words would trigger the explosion he was waiting for, the confession that he needed. Without breaking stride, he continued his attack. "Tell me what happened, Dane. Did Gail make contact with you while she was in prison? Did she plead her case to you about how she was set up? About how Josh betrayed her? Is that what pushed you over the edge? Did she lay a guilt trip on you about how you weren't there for her when she was growing up? About how you abandoned her? Was killing Josh your way of proving your love for your daughter?"

Dane's final hold on his control snapped. "Shut up! You don't have a clue about what happened. I wanted to be there for Gail. It was her mother who wouldn't let me. Did you think I wanted to see another man raise her? Have her call another man her father? I wanted to acknowledge Gail as my daughter, but her mother's family wouldn't let me. They didn't think I was good enough for their family. That I was worthy enough to raise Gail."

"So you killed Josh as a way of proving your worthiness," Jack charged, holding back his satisfaction at hearing Dane confirm his knowledge of his relationship to Gail. He knew if he wanted to get a full confession from the man, he couldn't allow anything or anyone distract him. At this time, at this second, Dane wasn't thinking rationally. He wasn't considering the consequences of his words. He was too wrapped up in the heat of the moment, too lost in the torment of his mind. Jack needed to make sure that he kept him on his present path of self-destruction. Ignoring Mitch, who was trying desperately to gain Dane's attention, he continued to confront Dane, hoping to break through the man's final walls of resistance. "Gail conned you into killing for her, didn't she? She played you for a fool. She wanted vengeance against Josh and she made sure you felt guilty enough at abandoning her to help her achieve her goal. She made sure you felt responsible for her downfall."

Dane leaped to his feet, his knuckles resting on top of the table, and he leaned threateningly toward Jack. "Josh deserved to die! My daughter's life is ruined because of him!" he exploded. "He was her acknowledged family. He should have protected her. All the talk and recriminations about my lack of parental qualifications, and the rest of the family couldn't do anything to save her. They stood on the sidelines while one of their own turned against her. While one of their own effectively stopped her life. Not a single one of them stepped in to help her. They all turned a blind eye. And I had to sit there and watch it happen. I watched as they met with Josh after Gail was arrested. I saw the way they forgave him, as if they understood why he did what he did. There was no loyalty for my daughter. Their sympathy was with Josh."

Jack never broke eye contact with Dane. "And you weren't going to tolerate that, were you? You killed Josh to even the score. Tell me, how easy was it? How much satisfaction did you get when you knew your plan had worked?"

Dane's eyes narrowed. "What exactly do you want me to say? That I got a high from killing Josh? That I enjoyed watching him die? Well, I hate to disappoint you, but the only thing I felt was relief. Relief that he could no longer hurt my daughter. Relief that the man was so predictable that I didn't have to go out of my way to accomplish what I needed to. He was a loner. I knew that he would eventually find himself working alone that night. That eventually the opportunity would present itself for me to slip the poison into his drink. It was so simple. All I had to do was keep an eye on him and wait for the man to fall into his routine," he ground out harshly, the full force of his anger consuming him.

Silence filled the room, and Mitch Stevens looked at Jack and Ryan. "I need to talk to my client in private," he said, visibly shaken by Dane's outburst.

After a long moment, Jack nodded and stood. "Of course," he said, knowing that there was nothing that the two of them could talk about that would make any difference in the prosecution of Dane Trevor for Josh Brody's murder. "We'll be right outside."

Ryan followed Jack. The moment they were on the other side of the door, he said, "You did good."

Jack ran a weary hand across the back of his neck. "Thanks. He held out longer than I thought he would. I wasn't sure for a while there if he would crack."

"I sensed the change in him when you mentioned murder one and the death penalty. That's when I think the reality of his situation hit him. He went into a complete tailspin at that point."

"Luckily it was one that his lawyer couldn't pull him out of."

"Yeah," Ryan agreed. "You should give Ed the news."

"You do it. I want to stay here and see this thing out."

"Are you sure?"

"Yes."

"All right. I'll catch up with you later."

"I'll be here."

Chapter Twenty-Four

Later that evening, Jack, Ashley, Ryan, and Jane sat across from one another at Palermo's. They were finally able to relax now that Josh Brody's murderer had been caught.

Jane took a sip of her water before resting a manicured hand against Ryan's suit sleeve. "I want to thank you all for your support during this time."

Ryan covered her hand with his and squeezed it reassuringly. "At least this is all behind us now."

"I know. I just can't believe that Dane Trevor murdered Josh. I mean the man seemed so normal. So kind."

Ashley smiled at her sympathetically. "I know better than anybody that people aren't always what they seem. It's hard when reality comes crashing in, pointing out people's faults and flaws with a neon light."

"Ain't that the truth," Ryan agreed.

"How did Josh's family take the news?" Jane asked.

Jack gave a small shrug. "Hard. Apparently they knew Dane when he was younger, but they knew him under a different name. It took awhile for them to make the connection."

"Different name?" Jane questioned.

"Yeah. The man's full name is Dane James Trevor, Jr., so in order to avoid confusion within his own family, he was called Jim. I guess the name stuck with him. Anyway, when Josh's family realized exactly who killed Josh, they were stunned. They had no idea of the connection that Dane shared with Gail Barret and her mother. As far as they knew, he was just a close family friend."

"This news must have devastated them," Jane said.

"It would devastate anyone," Ashley agreed as the waiter came to take their order and refill their water glasses.

After placing their orders, Ryan turned to Jane. "Do you know when the museum is going to reopen?"

Jane gave a slight shrug. "They're hoping sometime next week. They're going to have a dedication plaque placed outside the Egyptian exhibition honoring Josh's work for the museum."

Ashley smiled. "That sounds like a wonderful thing to do."

Jane returned her smile. "I agree. Josh put a lot of himself into the design of the exhibition. I think it's a fantastic way to acknowledge his contribution."

Ryan took a sip of water. "I'm just glad we were finally able to get a handle on what happened. At least the rest of our lives will be able to resume to normal."

"Amen to that," Jack muttered, placing a hand over Ashley's.

Ashley smiled and turned her hand in Jack's. Lifting her water glass, she said, "I'd like to propose a toast. To all of life's joys and sorrows. May they all make us more aware of just how wonderful life can be."

"I'll second that," Jane said, clinking her glass against Ashley's and waiting for Jack and Ryan to do the same.

After raising his glass, Ryan looked at Jack and Ashley. "And here's to good friends."